THE MEANING OF DEATH

JAMES L. CANNON

Abstract

Join Carter, Warden and Claire as they embark on a spiritual quest to explore that which awaits us all: death. It is your destiny, the great Archangel Michael has told them, to find and reveal for all humanity, the answers to the six epic questions:

1. WHAT IS THE MEANING OF HUMAN LIFE ON EARTH?

2. ARE HUMANS ETERNAL SOULS TRAPPED IN BODIES?

3. WHAT SPIRITUAL POWERS DO HUMANS POSSESS?

4. WHY ARE THERE, PAIN, SUFFERING, AND SICKNESS IN THE LIFE OF EVERY HUMAN BEING?

5. IS THERE A PARTICULAR WAY MODERN HUMANS SHOULD LIVE?

6. **WHAT IS THE MEANING OF DEATH?**

Each book in the series involves the answer to one of these questions with which our spiritual surveyors create a modern **Handbook of the Soul** containing fascinating insights into the meaning and purpose of human life, and most importantly what is expected of us while we are here.

Thousands of years of global philosophy, theology and science have been examined to find the credible purpose and meaning of human existence. Although the fictional stories surrounding it will entertain you, the handbook's real and rational answers to the timeless questions can help you see the true nature of your soul and the meaning of human life on earth.

Acclaim for the Series
Living as a Modern Soul in a Human Body

An author with an exceptional variety of life experiences has created an exciting series of short books addressing the fundamental questions of human existence.

Viewing life from the unique perspectives of a retired university vice president, a small city mayor, a corporate manager, an undercover intelligence operative, and a decorated military officer, Mr. Cannon provides a concise and thought-provoking account of the essential elements of wisdom necessary for us to thrive and grow.

The six stories, cover life's meaning, the keys to human happiness, and spiritual powers we can all claim, as well as the purpose of virtue, and morality. They also cover ways to encounter God, experience death and how to live well and die well.

The entertaining, six-book series--Living as a Modern Soul in a Human Body--was created to pass a very practical and valuable, body of moral, ethical and spiritual knowledge to future generations. However, I heartily recommend the series as a great and easy read for anyone interested in becoming all they can be while on this Earth.

Jerry L. Beasley
President Emeritus
Concord University

Table of Contents

Book 6

THE MEANING OF DEATH

Series

The following six serial books included in the series *Living as a Modern Soul in a Human Body* are best read in the following order*:

Book 1: *The Meaning of Life*

Book 2: *Souls Trapped in Bodies*

Book 3: *Human Spiritual Powers*

Book 4: *Why Human Suffering*

Book 5: *A Soul's Code of Conduct*

Book 6: *The Meaning of Death*

THE MEANING OF DEATH

Book 6 in the series

Living as a
Modern Soul in a Human Body

JAMES L. CANNON

Printed in the United States of America

ISBN 13-978-0-9968528-9-0

This book is dedicated to God the Father
Who created us
and sustains us

Scriptural verses from KJV

On the cover:
Renaissance genius Leonardo da Vinci's famous 1490 drawing the Vitruvian Man
(soul and apron added).

Introduction

This is the final book in a serial set of six books; this book covers fasting, physical contact with God, the meaning of death, what to expect in the dying process, an experience of death and how to die well.

The book also covers the most important Frequently Asked Questions (FAQs) about matters of the soul, and it includes the series bibliography for those interested in learning more about the topic.

The books in this series use an adventure story to convey vital spiritual truths about the human soul. Those truths are outlined in the Handbook of the Soul section of each chapter.

For clarity, **important points and concepts** are **repeated** and **expanded** from chapter to chapter. The spiritual intelligence in the Handbook of the Soul is presented in a bulleted outline format of thought-sized bites for easier, reading. A glossary of significant terms as used in this set of stories is located at the end of book one.

While acknowledging many and varied sources of information, it is the author who ultimately responsible for the content, and it is my earnest hope that these pages will help make life a little more meaningful for those whose eyes may chance upon them.

James L. Cannon
Soulsline9@gmail.com
08 October 2020

"Often when you think you're at the end of something,
you are at the beginning of something else."
...Fred Rogers

Chapter 1

<u>Fasting and Human Contact with God</u>

Hello, this is Doc and it will be my privilege to guide you through this chapter of our story. We were all amazed at Claire's unique experience at the end of book 5 when she got to see the Ten Commandments in the tabernacle over 3,000 years ago. Although, one young man named Carter, despite his efforts to hide it, was obviously quite jealous that he was not involved. In this chapter we begin the search for the answer to the last of our great questions of enduring importance:

WHAT IS THE MEANING OF DEATH?

At the conclusion of the previous book, my license to operate our medical clinic was suspended by the Socialist administration for refusing to treat unlimited numbers of government officials ahead of patients who had been waiting in line for days. We continued treating patients and meanwhile, the government established a heartless Health Assessment Review Board to limit care for the elderly who the government decides are no longer economically useful.

Not all storms come to disrupt your life.
Some come to clear a path.
...Anonymous

Chapter 1 Human Contact with God

We also received an invitation to go on an all expense paid vacation to an Inca holy site in Peru from our famous archeologist friend Dr. Jones. Today, we are considering our options with all the patients who still need our help, versus the overwhelming need for a break and the likelihood that the Socialist government will soon shut us down for operating without a license.

This morning Carter received a tip from a former patient, in a position to know, that next week the Socialists are planning to shut us down by putting all of us in handcuffs and hauling us off to jail with great fanfare and media coverage as a warning to all who refuse to collaborate with them. I have convened a meeting of the staff and we decide that we now have no choice but to accept Dr. Jones' invitation. We will lock up the clinic and the staff not going to Peru will go home for a break until things get sorted out.

On the flight to Peru, I explain that near the Inca holy city of Machu Picchu, Dr. Jones has found a dying 112-year-old Inca native who is said to be the descendant of a high priest who had knowledge of the ancient *Book of Living*. Jones wants me to try to keep the woman alive at least long enough to hear what she is trying to tell him about human contact with God.

We arrive at Lima International Airport, change planes to a small turboprop and fly high into the Andes Mountains to the old town of Cusco former capital of the Inca Empire. There we are treated to cocoa tea to help remedy the altitude sickness that assails many who are unaccustomed to the 11,000-foot elevation.

In 1492, when Columbus arrived in the New World, the wealthy Inca Empire extended along the pacific coast of South America for 2,500 miles, covering more than half the length of the continent and most of the Andes Mountain Range. A long highway network of roads and paths for runners connected the lengthy empire.

By 1572, Spanish conquistadors with horses, vastly superior weapons and armor had defeated all Inca armies, killed most of the ruling class and thoroughly looted the entire Incan empire.

The Meaning of Death

We are leaving Cusco on a creaky, old bus and starting the journey that will take us through pouring rain to the sacred Inca retreat still many miles away.

After 50 harrowing miles of narrow, muddy, winding mountain roads and hairpin curves, we finally arrive at a village at the foot of Machu Picchu on the bank of the fast-moving Urubamba River. There, the famous archeologist, Dr. Jones, is staying in an aged, mud-brick and stone dwelling with a leaky corrugated tin roof. A fire burns in a circle of stones on the worn dirt floor, while several native women look on.

In bed, is Jones' old Inca patient named Emmojean who is a short, frail woman, with lined, leathery, bronze skin, black eyes with thin, black hair and no teeth that testify to her advanced age. The light in her kind eyes is dim, and she tries to sit up and greet me, but she can barely speak a few raspy words of Spanish. Quetal, Emmojean I reply.

I check her physical vitals and detect the delicate pulse of her soul and some ideas come to mind that should help her. In a couple of days, Emmojean is feeling better, able to speak and willing to drink soup. I confide to Jones that the respite may be short and that I fear her end is near.

Jones then sits down beside the woman's bed with a digital voice recorder and asks Emmojean to explain what she knows about the mysterious *Book of Living*.

The old Inca says tradition has it that many centuries ago an ancient scroll arrived on the shores of the then prosperous Inca Empire. Jones asks her if she knows how it had arrived, but she does not.

Through the sound of endless rain hammering the metal roof, Emmojean goes on to say that since the book was written in a picture-word language foreign to the Inca, it was brought to the high priests at Machu Picchu to see if they could decipher it.

Temper gets you into trouble; pride keeps you there.
...Anonymous

According to legend, the Priests, after much effort, came up with an understanding of the document. Emmojean then repeats what she had been told by her grandfather about a process of fasting, withdrawal from everything and a deep look into one's self.

What she reveals is a means of personal training for those seeking any kind of divine contact prior to death. She describes five stages of human contact with Divine Power. Finally, she says that only those who live a life of extreme dedication and spiritual focus can have any hope for a personal encounter with holiness while still on earth.

The next day, in her last act on earth, the old one pulls from a dust covered trunk an ancient scroll wrapped in some kind of preserving leaves. The very well-worn papyrus scroll is sure enough in Egyptian hieroglyphics.

Jones is astounded, and he thanks her profusely. She says she is the last of her line, and she wants some good to come from the sacred knowledge that has been passed down to her. Later that night, she passes quietly away in her sleep, and the rain finally lets up.

Mia, Carter, Claire and Casey accompanied me on this trip and all are moved to tears when Emmojean is buried in a ceremony worthy of a queen. She was very popular in the town, having made many friends in her long life. The rocky, half washed out roadway to the burial ground is lined with thousands of silent people.

After the funeral, Jones takes all of us on a tour of the Incan temple complex of Machu Picchu. It is a 15th century Inca site unknown to the outside world until 1911. It may have been the Incas' last hiding place, as it was never found by the Spanish conquistadors.

Perched in the clouds, Machu Picchu sits on a mountain ridge high above the "Sacred Valley" 50 miles North of Cusco. It was a self-sufficient community with terraced fields on all sides of the steep ridge.

He that would have the fruit must climb the tree.
...Thomas Fuller

Mia and Casey are so impressed with all they have seen, that they volunteer to prepare a research report on Human Contact with God. They make the report on contact with God as it has evolved through time and on fasting, for it seems to be a prerequisite.

Mia says the surest way to learn the meaning of death would be to make contact with God and ask Him!

Jones sends me an English transcript of the recording he made of Emmojean's revelations and a translation of the scroll from the famous *Book of Living* that she gave him.

The thing that bothers Jones is that the 5,000-year-old first Egyptian dynasty usually associated with the "*Book of Living*" was so many millennia older than the Inca Empire of Machu Picchu and half a world away. Carbon dating puts the ancient scroll's origin in the period of the first Egyptian dynasty. So how did it get across so many centuries and so many miles? However, he noted in the Holy Bible there are references in Psalms to a heavenly *Book of the Living*.

After a great deal of research, Casey and Mia wrote the following report about fasting and human contact with supernatural Divinity:

Handbook of the Soul
Fasting and Divine Contact

I. Fasting

Fasting is a discipline that can help clarify your communications with Divinity. It shows, among other things, that you are committed and willing to sacrifice something to seek God's help. According to the book "Fasting for *Spiritual Break Through*" by Elmer L. Towns, there are at least eight different **purposes** for fasting and several different types of fasts.

Fasting is an aid to prayer, which in military parlance would be called a prayer force multiplier because it can multiply the effectiveness of any kind of prayer.

II. Eight Purposes for Fasting

1. To help free yourself or others from addictive behavior

2. To help solve difficult problems

3. To help get relief from problems that control your life

4. To help you meet humanitarian needs of others

5. To bring clearer insight and perspective when making important decisions

6. To help gain a healthier life or specific healing

7. To help you prepare for a special mission

8. To help bring you closer to Spiritual protection

III. Five Types of Fasts

1. **The Normal Fast:**

   - Doing without food for a specific period of time taking only water and juices

   - Normal fasting for more than a week should be attempted only with medical supervision.

2. **The Absolute Fast:**

   - Taking no food or water for a very limited period of time since many people would not survive three days without water or other liquids

   - A prior medical check-up and medical supervision are recommended for absolute fasts lasting longer than a day.

3. **The Partial Fast**:

- *Omits certain foods or meals for example, only vegetables or skipping lunch for a week*

4. **The Rotational Fast**:

- *Omitting various families of foods in rotation*

5. **The Voice Fast**:

Going for a day, a week or so without speaking. Observe its effect on you, and in your silence be more attuned to a spiritual connection with God.

- *It's an amazing tool for discovering what motivates our desire to speak. Often it is to get something from others like physical things but also approval, respect, understanding, gratitude, admiration or something else.*

- *If you reflect on why you want to say the things you are unable to say in a voice fast, it might reveal some interesting patterns and motivations to your conversations.*

- *You may find a pattern of listening to others to detect how to get what you want, or perhaps how to help others with what they want.*

- *This fast does require some understanding from family and friends. For strangers you just motion to your throat as if there is something wrong and you can't talk.*

Fasting can help break the bondage of besetting addiction, which is addiction you cannot break with normal willpower. Taking control of your desires by fasting can often help develop the discipline to get control of an addiction or other issues.

Most importantly, however, fasting interrupts our usual physically centered activities and puts us in a somewhat better position to sense matters of the spirit.

IV. Physical Benefits of Fasting Food

Rex Russell, MD notes that physical benefits from food fasts include healing and rest; rest for our digestive system from an overload of foods many of which are addictive and bad for our health. It is estimated that millions of people are negatively affected by the consumption of toxic substances.

*According to the Kellogg report: Food addiction is caused by affluent overloads of once rare substances from **nicotine** to **sugar** to **salt** to **caffeine** and **cocaine** that now flood our society. Two hundred years ago the average person consumed about 2 pounds of sugar per year. We now average over 150 pounds of sugar per person year.[1]*

Both eating disorders and emotions that go with them can be helped by proper fasting and prayer. Often food addictions require from three weeks to three months abstinence from the offending food to clear the brain's craving. If not controlled, unbridled consumption of harmful foods leads to gluttony, poor health and an epidemic of diabetes.

V. Keeping a Fasting Journal

It is recommended that we keep a journal while fasting to gain the most benefit from it. There is no rigid format to it you can just treat it as a diary.

Begin your journal by recording the date you start a fast, and then enter any insights that come to you or unusual circumstances you encounter. You can describe your emotions and any spiritual notions you might feel, as well as, the physical state of your body, i.e. rested, alert, tired, calm or agitated.

VI. Preparing to Fast

1. *Prepare for your fast with a "pre-launch check sheet" similar to the example on the following page:*

2. *State in **writing** the specific result you are seeking. This will focus and strengthen your will and energy on the solution. It will also solidify your faith to help generate expectation and anticipation of positive results, and a witness helps you remain accountable.*

Example Pre-Fast Commitment Sheet

Participant	John J. Doe
Aim	To lose weight
Affirmation	I am fasting because I want God's help in breaking the bondage of gluttony.
Vow	God being my strength, and grace being my basis, I commit myself to the fast outlined below.
Fast	I will abstain from all dessert foods and Soda Pop.
Period	Monday through Friday
Start Date	February 1st 2011
End Date	Good Friday 2011
Purpose	To get control over my diet and lose 20 lbs
Basis	Isa.58:6
Resources	None
Witnesses	Brenda Doe
Participant	Signature_____Date_____
Witness	Signature_____Date_____

Pre-Fast Commitment Form

Participant	
Aim	
Affirmation	
Vow	
Fast	
Period	
Start Date	
End Date	
Purpose	
Basis	
Resources	
Witnesses	
Participant	Signature_____Date_____
Witness	Signature_____Date_____

VII. Mysticism and Human Contact with God

Humans have reported glimpses of divinity and heavenly experiences that may be possible while still a human being. These events fall into a couple of categories:

*1. **Near Death Experiences** – As previously covered in book 2, people sometimes report out of body or near-death experiences at which times they see their bodies below them on the operating room of a hospital or on the shore after a frigid water drowning.*

- *While their body appears to be lifeless, they have, what they later recall, as a very brief heavenly or spiritual experience before returning to their human bodies.*

- *These are often categorized as Near-Death Experiences or NDEs.*

*2. **Mysticism** - There are also some historical reports of extremely dedicated religious people trying to find God through an experience generally known as Mysticism. Mysticism involves overcoming the central human focus on self to have a direct experience with the divine.*

*Mystics often use a process of **withdrawal** from contact with the outside world and a focus of introspection or a very deep look into their own souls to bring about physiological, psychological and spiritual transformation. A search for God may then take place through emanation or immanence.*

- ***Emanation** - assumes that God's presence is **outside** the human essence of man or woman. Therefore, the mystic's consciousness must travel upward and outward toward God.*

- ***Immanence** - by contrast, assumes that the shortest path to God lies through the interior of the human soul. In this case, the mystic must journey within to contact the divine spark of human creation.*

Regardless of religious perspective, most of us believe that there must be more to life than meets the eye.
... Author Kurt Bruner

*Although individual mystics are different, patterns in their reported journeys suggest **six stages** in their pilgrimage for a spiritual transformation via a direct encounter with God.*

1. *The first stage is an **awakening** and awareness that life, as they have been living it, is not right or complete, and a realization that they must turn their lives towards God.*

2. *The second stage is an effort to change their activities and to **purify their souls** as much as humanly possible to become worthy of some kind of contact with God.*

3. *The third stage of the mystic's pilgrimage is a brief flash, preview or **epiphany** of divine presence. It is said that many mystics are satisfied with having experienced the presence of God and never go beyond that stage.*

4. *The next stage can be a letdown feeling of abandonment as the soul yearns for more divine exposure.*

5. *Finally, after much perseverance, some are said to have reached the fifth stage, which is a **flash of union** or oneness with God. [2]*

   - *At this point, some mystics have claimed to be in the presence of God while maintaining their selfhood.*

   - *Others claim to have experienced spiritual union with the essential divine nature of God.*

6. *Such a state reportedly involves a deep mental alteration and often involves a physical trance during which the body appears to be lifeless. [3]*

"Suffering is the recoil of misdirected strength. We must make a point of uplifting and encouraging one another."
...Philosopher James Allen

Saint Francis of Assisi was reported to have had such a powerful mystical experience with Jesus that he was left with the "Stigmata," which are the same wounds verified on his body in the same places as those inflicted on Jesus during his crucifixion.[4]

*According to the early Christian mystics, the best means of **personal preparation**[5] for seeking the way to God requires the following:[6]*

- *Purging yourself of self-centeredness*

- *Continuous prayer that meditates on God*

- *Asceticism (living a spiritually clean, self-supporting simple life with few possessions and little money)*

- *Ethical self-discipline and control over human passions and desires*

- *Humility and service to others*

- *A forgiving and uncritical attitude toward others*

- *Love of neighbor as of self*

Ascetic monks and mystics of the fourth century wrote about the constant battle with the temptations of the following eight particular human vices: [7]

1. *Gluttony (overeating)*

2. *Impurity (lust)*

3. *Anger*

4. *Vainglory (excessive display of virtue for others)*

5. *Pride*

6. *Sadness*

7. *Despair*

8. *Avarice (greed)*

Those that succeeded in overcoming these temptations and seriously subscribed to the preparation noted above were successful candidates for a mystical experience. Evidently, such experiences were common enough to demonstrate that the mystical path to a divine experience was possible.

*Perhaps the best depiction of a mystical experience is that of the pragmatist philosopher William James. In his work, the "Varieties of Religious Experience," he noted the following **properties** of a mystical experience:*[8]

- **Ineffable** - They cannot be accurately described.

- **Noetic** - They convey a deep sense of truth or knowledge.

- **Transitive** - They can occur only for a short time.

- **Passive** - They cannot be willed to occur.

Over the ages, very few mystics have shared their experiences in writing, making it difficult to estimate their rates of success. According to Doctor Rick Strassman, the features of a mystical experience include: [9]

1. *The three pillars of self, time and space undergo a profound change in appearance that reveals great beauty and spirituality.*

2. *Personal identity disappears, as all of existence seems to become one.*

3. *Past, present and future merge into the timeless existence of eternity.*

4. *Space becomes vast without boundary, and here and there are in the same place.*

5. *The mystic realizes the certainty of life after human death.*

6. *Powerful feelings of joy and intense bliss surge through the mystic's consciousness with an underlying sense of peace.*

7. *There may be a searing sensation of the sacred and holy if one approaches too close to the unimaginably powerful white light of God.*

8. *An encounter with the intensely powerful, wise and loving God of creation that may leave one with an enlightened ability to understand human life.*

Return to human existence seems to involve the pure energy of the soul's consciousness slowing in frequency to an earthly rate of vibration and thus reentering their physical bodies.

In his book The Spiritual Brain: Science and Religious Experience[10], neuroscientist Dr. Andrew Newberg notes the following:

- *"There are certain religious and spiritual experiences that might be considered the pinnacle of self-transcendence (the going beyond the limit of self).*

- *"These mystical experiences—sometimes called salvation or enlightenment—are a powerful source of self-transcendence.*

- *"The experience is frequently perceived as the person changing into an entirely new state of being.*

- *"Associated with these mystical experiences are changes in the bodies' nervous systems.*

- *"Mystical states appear to be associated with profound changes in the autonomic nervous system."*

For all mystics, the meaning of life is to be found in the journey toward God. Their approach to advancing that journey varies somewhat by individual.

However, the common aspects of their journeys noted above seem to point to a life of extreme dedication and prayerful spiritual focus as prerequisites for any hope of an early encounter with the Spirit of Divine Consciousness.

- *In spite of the increasingly secular nature of western culture, mysticism continues to attract advocates who are trying to pierce the veil and transcend the cloud of unknowing that exists between man and God.*

- *The daily world we perceive with our five senses is not enough to discover God and the truth of ultimate reality, so mystics dig deeper into the transcendent world of spirit.[11]*

Modern religion seems more interested in transforming the world rather than transcending it. Technology, commerce and communications have yielded a worldview that is profoundly materialistic, competitive and secular. Unfortunately, many people have lost concern for other people in a preoccupation with themselves.

Yet for mystics, there is still a hunger for something more than the values and practices of a material existence, the desire for something more real than what is available in modern culture.

Modern mystics might be seen as spiritual scouts reporting on realities more real than our worldly experiences.

VIII. Summary

The best means of deserving a way to God include:

- *Unselfishness*
- *Fasting and prayer*
- *A simple unstressed lifestyle*
- *Ethical self-discipline and control over human passions*
- *Humility and service to others*
- *A forgiving and uncritical attitude toward others*
- *Love of neighbor as of self*

I am quite proud of the research paper written by Mia and Casey, so I ask Carter to make copies for all the staff and one for his book, which is shaping up to be a modern "Book of Life."

Carter keeps a record of all the seminars and more in their handbook of the Soul. Warden decides to take a copy of this report to their old friends the Ascetics just in case any of the material was unknown to them.

The Meaning of Death

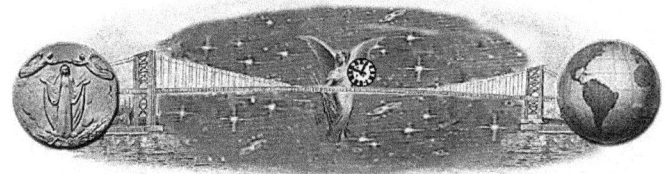

Prayer and love are bridges across time and space.

<u>A Little Perspective on Time</u>

A **million** seconds was ---12 **days** ago

A **billion** seconds was ---32 **years** ago

A **trillion** seconds was ---32,000 **years** ago

While we were in Peru, the Socialist administration passed the Religious Activity Act that requires all religious organizations to register with the government and to obtain a permit to engage in religious activity of any kind. It also restricts the size of all individual houses of worship meaning churches, synagogues, mosques etc to a maximum of 50 members each. In addition, the law forbids public prayer and eliminates religious programs on electronic broadcast media.

Polls show that Socialism is most unpopular among families that profess religious beliefs. Therefore, the justification for the Religious Activity Act is that religion is unpatriotic and a danger to the country. It is probably just a matter of time until they prohibit organized religion altogether.

Carter received an email from the administration reinstating my medical license saying that our duty to the nation can now be met by seeing only a dozen Socialist officials per day ahead of other patients. Our source in the administration says this is due to Socialism's growing unpopularity, the worsening shortage of food, medical service and even toilet paper and the fact that the next elections are less than a year away.

Human life is meant for a little austerity. We have to purify our existence to get spiritual realization; that is the mission of human life.
...A.C. Bhaktivedanta

Chapter 1 Human Contact with God

Uncontrollable outbreaks of Typhus, Plague and Ebola are rumored to be killing millions of people due to the shortage of medical care.

The news media under government control continues to report great satisfaction with Socialism and even enthusiasm for the Socialist administration and its policies, but everyone knows that's a joke.

We decide to reopen the clinic, not to fill out the health assessments forms on our older patients and to do what we can to help defeat the socialist party in the next election.

I have been asked how the Socialist party ever got elected in the first place. I realize I am probably the only one at the clinic that knows the history of Socialism and how badly it's failed everywhere it's been tried.

If you haven't witnessed it, it's hard to imagine how hundreds of years of economic progress can be destroyed by a few years of Socialism. Socialism eliminates the powerful personal economic incentives of capitalism that motivate productivity and generate prosperity. Socialism also leaves too much power in the hands of the government, and that power eventually corrupts officials, until people can get ahead only by serving corrupt government officials instead of one another.

Socialism has always led to dictatorship, loss of personal and religious freedom, economic breakdown and poverty. According to Frank Dikötter, a Hong Kong-based historian, Chinese communist party records show that from 1958 to 1962 at least 45 million people were worked, starved or beaten to death in China. This, because the Socialist country's leader, Mao Zedong, tried to force the population to catch up economically to Capitalist countries in a devastating program known as the "Great Leap Forward."

In his book *Mao's Great Famine, The Story of China's Most Devastating Catastrophe,* Dikötter notes that for those who committed any acts of disobedience toward the Socialist government, however minor, the punishments were huge. State retribution for tiny thefts, such as stealing a potato, even by a child, would include being tied up and thrown into a pond; parents were forced to bury their children alive; people were doused in excrement and urine, others were set on fire, or had a nose or ear cut off.

One record shows how men were branded with red-hot irons. People were forced to work naked in the middle of winter. In one region, two hundred thousand Chinese villagers were banned from the official feeding facilities because they were too old or ill to be effective workers, so they were deliberately starved to death.[12]

According to the authoritative "Black Book of Communism," overall an estimated 65 million Chinese died because of Mao's repeated, merciless attempts to create a new "socialist" China. Anyone who got in his way was done away with by execution, imprisonment or starvation.[13]

Socialism stifles individual freedom and initiative and crushes the power and creativity of the human spirit. History shows that Socialism has been tried and failed in 27 countries[1]. In every case, it has proven to be an economic and human disaster kept in force only by dictators. Keeping it in force has required using secret police, making people spy on one another, even using children to spy on their parents, and using military force including tanks and other armored military vehicles against protestors as in Hungary, China and Venezuela.

Our situation under Socialism continues to worsen. Here at the base camp clinic, we still strive to be positive and all pray for relief while struggling to cope with its depressing economic consequences. There are shortages of everything including medicine and surgical supplies for our patients.

Fortunately, we were able to smuggle some critical medications back from Peru hidden in souvenirs. We are now using well washed clothing for bandages and boiling and reusing needles and surgical supplies. Adding insult to injury is the increasingly pompous arrogance of the Socialist officials that expect to be treated like royalty when they know

---

[1] Former Socialist countries: Russia, Ukraine, Byelorussia, Uzbekistan, Kazakhstan, Georgia, Azerbaijan, Lithuania, Latvia, Estonia, Moldavia, Kirghizia, Tajikistan, Turkmenia, Armenia, Albania, Bulgaria, Czechoslovakia, East Germany, Hungary, Poland, Croatia, Macedonia, Montenegro, Serbia, Slovenia and Bosnia and Herzegovina. As of this writing, China, Cuba, North Korea, Vietnam, Laos and Venezuela remain Socialist under repressive communist dictators. China and Vietnam have reformed their economies with Capitalism.

we are desperate even for band-aids for the thousands of patients waiting to be seen.

Unwilling to trust our home-made bandages, they are starting to bring their own with them. Several have bragged that they have a warehouse of medicine and medical supplies for the private use of government officials.

----

[1] https://www.dhhs.nh.gov/dphs/nhp/documents/sugar.pdf 2021

[2] Teresa of Avila, *The Life of Saint Teresa of Avila*, London: Penguin Books, 1957.and John of the Cross, *Dark Night of the Soul*, New York: Image (numerous editions)

[3] Underhill, Evelyn. *Mysticism*, London: 1924 (Image: 1970, reprint)

[4] Johnson, Luke T. *Mystical Tradition,* The Teaching Company 2008 Lectures 15 &16

[5] Ibid re Lecture 15 - *Sayings of the Desert Fathers & John Cassian*

[6] Friedrich Heiler, *The History of Religions*, Chicago, Chicago University Press, 1959, pp. 142-53

[7] Johnson, Luke T. *Mystical Tradition,* The Teaching Company, 2008 Lecture 16 - Ivagrius Ponticus et al

[8] Johnson, David Kyle. *The Big Questions of Philosophy* – Course guidebook, The Teaching Company 2016, Lecture 10 – Can Mystical Experience Justify Belief? p.71

[9] Strassman, Rick M.D. - *DMT the Spirit Molecule* –Park Street Press © 2001p.234

[10] Newberg, Andrew M.D. *The Spiritual Brain: Science and Religious Experience* - ©The Teaching Company 2012 p.146-148

[11] Johnson, Luke T. *Mystical Tradition*–The Teaching Company 2008 Lecture 36 – Mysticism in the West Today

[12] www.independent.co.uk/arts-entertainment/books/news/maos-great-leap-forward-killed-45-million-in-four-years-2081630.html 09/17/2010

[13] www.heritage.org/asia/commentary/the-legacy-mao-zedong-mass-murder 2/2/2010

Chapter 2

<u>Death and Dying</u>

There is a time for everything
and a season for every activity under heaven,
a time to be born and a time to die.
(Ecclesiastes 3:1-2)

Hi, this is Casey, and it's my turn to be your guide. Six months have passed since the adventure at Machu Picchu, and we have settled back into our difficult life under Socialism. Claire has learned medicine quickly under Doc's expert supervision. Nevertheless, the shortages of drugs and supplies, are making it difficult to keep up with the now endless line of patients.

Carter and Claire have become soul mates, never seeming to tire of one another's company. I am tending a roof top garden, when on the radio I hear that a very rare tidal wave or tsunami has come ashore along the mid-Atlantic region of the U.S. east coast, not a day's drive from our location.

News reports are saying that casualties are heavy, prompting grave concern about the safety of our friends and relatives living on the coast. All at once, we start expressing our concerns aloud. We try making phone calls, but the circuits are overloaded and cellular systems are probably damaged or destroyed. We are wondering what, if anything, we can do to help.

The Meaning of Death

Warden suggests we turn the base camp into a small emergency hospital for badly injured kids. Doc likes the idea, as does everyone else. Warden is soon advising emergency management personnel that we are available to handle 30 to 40 children in serious condition.

The tidal wave causes various stages of damage and casualties in three states that are declared disaster areas. What remains of local medical facilities is being inundated with victims, and a system is set up to fly them to the already congested hospitals further inland.

Young casualties accumulate quickly at the base camp, and the full staff is soon working 16 hours a day seeing to the kids. In addition to the injured youngsters, we are seeing only the critical cases from the long line of our regular patients. We create a makeshift hospital ward to handle at least 40 patients either waiting for surgery or recovering.

Unfortunately, we are unable to save many young children. At times, various members of the team just break down and cry to cope with the tragedy of so many dead, dying and disfigured kids.

Finally, it begins to let up, and we find ourselves with a number of youngsters who have no remaining relatives and no place to go. Lynn, a cute, green-eyed, blonde sixteen-year-old with a pale complexion dies on the operating table despite Doc's very best and lengthy efforts to revive her, so she is put in the makeshift morgue. Much later, while I am counting corpses in the cool, dim basement, Lynn suddenly starts shrieking wildly in her high-pitched voice, scaring me half to death. Lynn recovers well noting only that she had a life changing experience.

Since she has no one to return to, Lynn remains at the home base compound for quite a while. The team is becoming very fond of her, especially since she gladly pitches in and makes it her business to help recovering children cope. This morning I ask Lynn about her experience while being clinically dead for so long.

"One of the marvels of the world is the sight of a soul sitting in prison with the key in its hand"
...Rumi

Chapter 2 Death and Dying

She responds saying, "Well at first I was like a free spirit, outside my body, but I couldn't figure out how I was moving. Then I realized it was by thought, just by thinking left right, up or down forward or backward. It was so cool.

"Just as I was having fun doing aerial acrobatics, I was pulled into some kind of cloud tunnel. I can't remember exactly what happened in the tunnel, but when I came out, I was in a body like this one again. It was somehow different though, lighter, brighter and well maybe, I felt aglow in it or something like that.

"I had arrived at a strange place. There seemed to be millions of people there, living a dull existence in drab, old low-income type housing projects for as far as the eye could see. We were all wearing the same sort of long, formless gray toga like robes.

"I asked where I was, and was told that I was in an entire dimension of these housing projects. It was all in black and white with no color, and there was nowhere else to go. Neither food nor drink was needed nor existed. However, someone said there was a trans-dimensional elevator to the upper dimensions that occasionally came by to take people up to the higher levels of heaven and bring them back if they didn't want to stay.

"Why, I asked them, would someone not want to stay in heaven's highest levels?"

'You just try going up there yourself and see how it fits with you,' one thin, older woman said to me.

"Will they keep me out?" I asked.

'No, dear, you are the only one that will keep you out, but no one wants to be where they know they don't fit in.'

"Do they think they are better than everyone else? I asked.

"One tall, thin, balding man with short, gray hair and a mustache said with a soft voice that his dad was in the highest heaven and had met him at the upper stop many times trying to get him to stay."

The Meaning of Death

"According to his dad, the concept of being better than someone else doesn't even exist there. They can't understand why not everyone wants to stay.

"He said," 'My dad told me that higher heavens can **greatly fulfill virtuous souls.** The highest **Heaven's** extremely holy atmosphere **can fulfill to the highest degree** the souls who on earth developed a largely **virtuous character**.'

'However, it can do nothing for those with serious character flaws or less than virtuous character in general. Therefore, because of our less virtuous values, convictions and thought habits we simply cannot be fulfilled in upper heaven, and we all find ourselves, for one reason or another, too uncomfortable to stay there.'

'God wants you with him in the highest dimension,' "his dad told him," 'and his grace offers everyone the chance, but the point is if your soul is not ready, the upper reaches would not seem to be heaven to you, even if you were there.'

'Even if souls of poor character are now seeking the good in some sense, their character will have developed on earth in such a less favorable direction, (away from a desire for goodness and virtue) that it leaves them unwilling and unable to flourish in the upper heavens,' "he said."

"Slowly getting the picture, I said, you mean people with weaker faith in the Trinity and less well-developed character would not find upper heaven to be a place they like."

'I am afraid so,' "he responded," 'I think our spiritual character must have stronger faith and goodness to be able to participate in the eternal, divine existence of love and positive energy that forms the upper dimensions of heaven.'

'Unreformed souls of weak faith and poor character are as out of place there, as fish out of water. Thus, we are unwilling and unable to exist in any of the other dimensions of heaven.'

Life has two extremes, one of laughter one of anguish.
...Anonymous

Chapter 2 Death and Dying

'I hate to admit it, but the barrier is entirely within us. For me it's like a deep, all-encompassing inferiority complex that keeps me feeling like I just don't belong anywhere else. So, it is, therefore, truly me keeping myself down here on this lower level of heaven,' "said the gray-haired man." 'On earth, I just ignorantly squandered my opportunity to develop virtuous character,' "he noted with regret," 'even though I did come to enough faith late in life to be admitted this far into heaven.'

"A short, anxious woman in dark glasses added," 'The only way to get a character virtuous enough to belong and feel comfortable in the company of the upper heavens is to have the faith to put yourself through another life on earth. However, who wants that, since you could end up with a lousy character, a less virtuous soul than the one with which you started, and no faith at all. Then, without enough faith, you would never even make it back to this level!'

"Does anyone ever try going back to earth? I Asked."

'Yes, oh yes, all the time,' "she said," 'and many are known to have moved up, but as far as we know, some never return at all. It is said that before every trip back to earth your memory for other reasons is suspended, so you really don't know if you are there for a repeat trip or not.'

'Apparently everything depends on having the courage and the will power to use the circumstances of an earthly existence to sufficiently improve your soul. To reach the highest realm, you must have complete faith and become virtuous enough to exist with God. Otherwise, once you have enough faith to get into heaven, you go only as high as your virtue will take you,' "said she."

"Well, asked I, If God so loves us all, why can't He change the rules so you can get in to the top dimension as well as anyone else?"

'I imagine it's because everyone there trusts everyone else not to create discord with negative attitudes and dishonorable conduct like lying, cheating and stealing. Letting dishonorable, unreformed souls in the upper heavens could undo the trust and harmony, reintroduce suspicion and make upper heaven over in the image of earth,' "said the gray-haired man."

The Meaning of Death

'In addition, as I understand it,' "he said," 'God's holiness, his very essence, is lethal to selfishness, disbelief and sin. Therefore, he has options for souls of weaker character, like us, that for our benefit, keep us safely separated from him.'

'There are the various levels of heaven, like this one full of people with barely adequate faith, and poor character with similar flaws that are stuck in the same dimension with one another. Here, one of the character flaws we all share is a negative attitude.'

'My dad says, God grants and respects human freedom to choose, therefore, he will not dictate our character to us. Neither will He force change on those unsuited to Him.[1] The community of souls on the top level is said to be composed of those who love God deeply, care about morality and goodness, and who labored tirelessly on earth to become souls of faith, honor and virtue.'

"Well, if you understand all that, why don't you go back to earth and get it right this time? I asked."

"He replied," 'Knowing how something works and doing it are two very different things. But, maybe I will someday,' "he said." 'Maybe I will go back to earth and fill my soul with so much virtue that they won't be able to stand me up there.'

'Of course, I would forget my motive by the time I got to earth. I would have to start all over trying to figure out why I was there and what I was supposed to do. And then, it would be my luck to make the same poor choices all over again or maybe even worse,' "he lamented."

"Not me, I said. I am going to make more virtuous choices every chance I get, even if I don't remember any of this."

'That very difference in attitude is why you will not fail, and I will not succeed,' "said the gray-haired man, who added," 'I have tried to shed this negative attitude that has plagued me for as long as I can remember, but I guess I am just too comfortable with it.'

"If God adds another day to our life, let us receive it gladly."
...Roman Philosopher Marcus Seneca

Chapter 2 Death and Dying

"The next time the trans-dimensional elevator came, I jumped aboard," Lynn said, "and I was soon in high heaven, and heavenly it was. There was a spectacular, nearly overwhelming atmosphere of intense goodness and love. It was truly stepping out of drab black and white into dazzling full color. Even the air seemed extra rich and wholesome.

"The fabulous sensation of everything was so vivid and appealing that my senses were stunned at first. People I knew and loved like my mother Jean were there begging me to stay. She looked so beautiful in a stylish, flowing white robe that was as light as a feather with a golden wrap around the waist and golden sandals. So, of course I wanted to stay, but I felt like I wasn't quite where I belonged -- not yet anyhow.

"It felt sort of like finding yourself at an elegant, formal party for which you are way under-dressed. It was as if all my friends were in ball gowns and tuxedos, and I was in blue jeans and cowboy boots.

"You want to stay and have a good time, but you also want to get home and get properly attired, except that I perceived the proper attire to be a matter of character not clothing. I felt an uncomfortable, sense of being out of place.

"A being of very bright light approached me but remained at a distance. Instantly, I felt a rush of ultimate love, peace and a deep sense of security all wrapped about me as if it were a warm blanket. His face shone like the sun, and his clothes were as white as light. I sensed the lord's glorious inter-essence of pure virtue and love within his translucent body like colored lightening moving about in slow motion.

"With the kindest voice I ever heard, he said 'you are not yet ready, my child, you still have important advancement to undergo on earth. Your time will come, and make sure when it does that you are properly attired in an elegant and gracious character before the transformation you call death.'"

"The next thing I knew," said Lynn, "I woke up in the cold, gloomy morgue with a sheet over me. You know, it's getting harder and harder to remember that experience. It's become like a slowly fading dream."

"Wow," says Mia, "that's quite an experience! You really should write that down before you forget it." Mia adds that Lynn's experience reminds her of a book called *"The Great Divorce"* by one of her favorite authors C.S. Lewis.

When things finally get back to the new normal, Warden tells us we have saved the lives of 256 young people and children hurt in the Tsunami. Unfortunately, we could not save 57 children including six infants. However, our line of regular patients camped out along the road sides is now about a quarter mile long.

There has been so much death and dying that Doc decides to try to restore morale a little by doing a seminar on Death and Dying. He hopes that having a better understanding of death will make it a little less forbidding to our team.

The seminar is presented on the following pages:

Handbook of the Soul

Death and Dying

I. Preview

All human beings go through the experience of death, usually as a result of the body's physical aging process.

- *Dying is the process of transitioning from the land of the dying to the land of the living, from this dimension to another.*

- *The event will mark the end of this opportunity to fashion, in the crucible of human life, a strong, virtuous spiritually based relationship with the divine order.*

II. Introduction

As family members and friends, we pass through this world hand in hand, seeing life come into the world as babies and grandbabies, and seeing it go out again as the light in the eyes of our parents and grandparents dims and departs.

The concept of death includes the following sub concepts:

1. **Universality** - *all living things die.*

2. **Irreversibility** - *the dead cannot return themselves to this life.*

3. **Non-functionality** - *all physical life functions end with death.*

4. **Causality** – *death can result from internal or external causes.*

5. **Existentiality** - *adult humans understand that one way or another they will eventually cease to exist in this dimension.*

You probably won't know in advance exactly how or when your body will die. Healthy children are usually at least ten years of age or older before they fully comprehend the concept of death.[2]

- *Most people transition from this life in hospitals, hospices or at home because of a serious illness.*

- *Some people depart suddenly in accidents, natural disasters, wars or as a result of crime.*

- *Sudden, unexpected departure can also result from heart failure or other medical emergencies.*

Just as there was the perfect time to be born, for our soul's energy to enter the earthly dimension, there is also the right time to leave. At that time, the spirit and soul are released from the body without having to endure the final pain of the body's physical decay.

III. The Meaning of Death

*Death adds value to life because in life's brief time span each remaining moment becomes more precious. Death is also the ultimate deadline. For some people, death's approach gradually provides motivation and a growing sense of urgency to determine what is important in life and a limited time frame for acting on it. You might ask yourself what you would have to do in your remaining time in order to get to your death bed feeling satisfied that you had **found, experienced, expressed and offered the best of yourself in this life**?*

We have a limited time in which to achieve a virtuous character of personal excellence and in which to help improve the social networks in which we live. We have a limited opportunity to ensure that it can be said of us when we are gone: "It was better that he was here or that she made a difference in the lives of others, and she did so happily, generously, creatively and compassionately."

"Realizing our lives have a finish line sealing our fate should help motivate us to become the souls we need to be."[3] When all is said and done, our lives should be a grand story or work of art that was well worth creating!

Socrates, one of the wisest men in human history, is quoted as saying that death might not be so bad. He states that "Being dead is one of two things: either the dead are nothing, as it were, and have no awareness whatsoever of anything at all; or else, as we're told, it's some sort of change, a migration of the soul from here to another place." If we no longer exist, we won't even know it; but if our souls do migrate to another dimension, we should try to be deserving of yet a better place than this.[4]

The leading cause of death is old age, but don't resent growing old. Many are denied the Privilege.

In another way of thinking the great scholar, Zhuangzi, said "death is the completion of life; life is difficult and the function of death is to give us a break from that toil—to give us rest." The implication of rest assumes when the rest is over, we are back to some other kind of challenging existence. [5]

IV. Leading Causes of Death

- *The annual death rate per 1,000 people is a mortality measure that varies widely by country due to demographics, health care and lifestyle.*

- *According to an early 21st century World Fact Book the world's average annual human death rate per 1,000 people was 8.87 or a little less than 1% per year.*

- *The highest death rate was in the African nation of Botswana with over 29 deaths per thousand people.*

- *The lowest death rate was in the Northern Mariana Islands at 2.3 per thousand people*

- *North America was near the middle at 8.25.*

Listed below are the five leading causes of death in most developed countries and their percentage of the total causes of death.[6]

Cardiovascular Disease	*29%*
Cancer	*23%*
Stroke	*7%*
Emphysema	*5%*
Accidents	*4%*

- *Poor diet and lack of exercise are the human behavioral influences that contribute most to heart and artery disease, which is the leading cause of death.*

- *Tobacco use is the human behavior that contributes most to cancer, which is the second most common cause of death.[7]*

- *According to the World Health Organization, more than 15 billion cigarettes are smoked each day by over 1.25 billion smokers worldwide, and about 5 million smokers die from illness related to this addiction each year.[8]*

- *Suicide is the 11th most common cause of death at 1.3%, and homicide or murder is 14th at 0.7%.*

- *Accidental deaths are the third leading cause of death for men, and the seventh leading cause of death for women.*

*The five leading types of **accidental** death in most developed countries and their percentage of the total accidental deaths are listed in the following table:[9]*

Motor vehicle accidents	44.3%
Falls	17.8%
Poisoning	13.0%
Drowning	3.9%
Fires	3.4%

The top five types of accidental death have remained the same for over 30 years, and they account for 80% of all accidental fatalities.[10]

- *Motor vehicle accidents kill 30,000 to 45,000 human beings each year and injure nearly three million.[11]*

- *They are the single leading cause of death for humans up to 29 years of age.*

- *The motor vehicle death rate is highest among the 15 to 24 age group.*

I intend to live forever, or die trying.
...Comedian Groucho Marx

- *A 16-year-old has 3 times the fatal crash risk of an 18-year-old and 7 times that of a 25-year-old.*

- *Almost half of all traffic fatalities are due to the influence of alcohol, and most of the rest are the result of driver fatigue.[12]*

V. Coping with Death

The vast majority of human beings believe in some form of life after death.[13] Doing so should certainly make coping with your demise a lot easier, unless of course, you think you are going to hell.

If you find you are dying from a terminal disease, you are likely to come to terms with it over a period of time by going through many or all of the following frequently overlapping stages:[14]

1. **Denial** – *As you might expect, facing death is not easy, and it takes some time to adjust to it.*

   - *Human beings often react to the news of their impending death with shock, disbelief and an inability to accept it.*

   - *Initial denial is a useful way to buy some of the time needed to come to grips with the prospect of our own death.*

2. **Anger** - *Once denial is no longer possible, an angry, resentful, bitter stage may set in during which we can become difficult to deal with.*

3. **Bargaining** – *The next stage of adjustment could be an effort to get God to give us an extension in return for living a better life or whatever else we think might work.*

4. **Depression** - *If we realize there is no denying our terminal condition, and we are weary of anger and cannot strike a bargain to gain time, we often become depressed.*

5. **Acceptance** – *The final stage of adjustment to our own death is one of acceptance, when we realize it is unavoidable, and that we are going to have to deal with it sooner rather than later.*

The Meaning of Death

Throughout their ordeals, it is not unusual for dying people to maintain hope for new medicine, a remission in their condition or divine healing. It is best not to diminish their hope, as it is an important part of the coping process.

It is usually easier for people to deal with the news of a terminal diagnosis while they are still relatively strong, and death is not yet eminent.

Death from terminal illness can take place fairly soon, or it can be a lengthy and emotionally difficult process.

Some people come to a final acceptance of their impending departure with little assistance, while others need help in working through the different stages in order to die in peace and dignity.

It is important to realize that the dying person needs as much encouragement, security and support as possible given the experience he or she is facing.

Some difficult choices concerning medical intervention often have to be made in the final stage of a human life.

These decisions should be made in the best interest of the terminally ill patient, but too often, they are made in the interest of family members who don't want to let their loved one go.

The end-of-life decisions can mean the difference between allowing someone to transition in peace and grace or prolonging their suffering by keeping them alive with tubes and machines.[15]

While you are still in good health, be sure to make your own preference on these matters known. Choose whom you want to make decisions for you with a simple "medical power of attorney" form. Forms are available online or at most hospitals and some doctor's offices.

**What a caterpillar calls the end of the world,
the Master calls a butterfly.**
...Richard Bach

Chapter 2 Death and Dying

Hospice *offers personal, gentle and respectful care and cost–efficient community-based services to human beings nearing the end of their lives and to those who love them. Hospice palliative care to alleviate pain is available at home, in a hospice facility or in designated hospice sections of hospitals.*

Hospicelink *has been a toll-free telephone information and referral service with a sympathetic, knowledgeable person who is ready to listen to your concerns.*

At the time of this writing, the number was **(800) 331-1620**, *and the Hospice Education Institute web site was* www.hospiceworld.org.

According to the Hospice Education Institute, hospice care neither shortens nor lengthens life. It offers a more peaceful passing and provides support for those who are left to grieve.

Veteran Hospice Social Worker Nancy Jacob has the following nine pieces of advice for those who may be dealing with an end-of-life situation:

1. People given a terminal diagnosis often talk about establishing a legacy or about how they want to be remembered and what impact they might have on their immediate community or the need to take care of unfinished business.

2. Substance abusers often have a need for higher doses of opioids due to a built-up tolerance.

3. Advance Medical Directives can avoid expensive, unwanted medical procedures

4. Depending on where you live, it can be important to have a Last Will and Testament on record at your county courthouse.

5. Registration with a Memorial Society can sometimes reduce funeral costs significantly.

**A reporter asked a 104-year-old woman
what she thought was the best thing about being so old.
"No peer pressure," she replied**

6. Pain killers especially opioids *can be your enemy during life but your friend at the end. Family members are sometimes apprehensive about your addiction to pain killers. However, if a doctor has given you a specific diagnosis for a life limiting illness of six months or less, it is important to request information about the symptoms you can expect and the appropriate pain killers to keep you from experiencing undue levels of pain and agony.*

7. Terminal agitation is a little understood phenomenon that often occurs about 72 hours before a patient (usually with a longer-term illness) passes away. Anxiety, physical agitation and restlessness are typically accompanied by a spike in the individual's temperature. Medication can help alleviate the symptoms.

8. If the deceased has passed away at home, it is respectful to position the body flat on their back in a bed with eye lids closed, perhaps a scarf over the head and under the jaw to hold their mouth closed and hands folded across their abdomen until professional personnel arrive.

9. The hardest thing for most people seems to be watching their loved one's body being carried out of the home for the last time.

Life is real! Life is earnest, and the grave is not the goal.
Dust thou art, to dust returnest, was not spoken of the soul!
... Poet H. Wadsworth Longfellow

__Rite of Passage__ - As a spiritual event of the greatest significance, your death will be a rite of passage that should result in the advancement of your soul as you transition from this life into the next dimension of your existence.

- *You might want to designate in advance those whom you would prefer to have present and whom you might like to have holding your hands when you depart this world.*

- *You could also request that a particular verse or short poem be read as or just before, you depart with your choice of music playing quietly in the background.*

- *If you are awake and conscious through the transitioning process, goodbyes can be exchanged and prayers offered as circumstances permit.*

Writing in his nineties, the famous evangelist Billy Graham related a friend's observation that people seem either to get better or to get bitter, as they grow older.

- *As we near home, we should seek God's help to learn not only what it means to grow older, but also to learn to grow older with grace and find the guidance needed to finish well.[16]*

- *One way to finish well, says Graham, is to pass on our highest values and our faith to those who follow us.[17]*

VI. Dying Well

In February 1779, Lieutenant Colonel __George Rogers Clark__ was an American Revolutionary War leader with a small force of militia who was assigned the near impossible job of taking a well-defended British fort at Vincennes in the middle of winter.

- *The British surrendered without a shot after witnessing the brutal execution of their recently captured Ottawa Indian allies purposefully staged in front of the fort.*

- *In an effort to intimidate the fort's defenders, Clark had the kneeling Indians executed with tomahawk blows to the head.*

- *After the first Indian was executed, the other Ottawa began to sing their death songs to make peace with their maker.*

It is said that the Ottawa Chief Makuk Mong then had a tomahawk blade sunk in his skull, whereupon he calmly removed it, with his bound hands, and returned it to his executioner who then finished the job.

That was a courageous way to die well, if ever there was one.

Most of us will never face such a terrible end; however, we may very well find ourselves facing a slow and difficult demise from the ravages of terminal disease.

- *The best we could do to "die well" would be to try to go out facing the transition with faith and courage.*

- *We should unselfishly try to make our passing as easy as possible on loved ones who are concerned about us and on the medical professionals giving us care.*

*All of us will face death. But, **how will we die**? Full of fear, resistance and terror, or will we go **courageously** and **gallantly** into eternity powered by God's gifts of **faith** and **grace**?* [18]

In his book Dying Well, Dr. Ira Byock noted that patients who died most peacefully appeared to be those who enjoyed active family relationships that included discussions of personal and spiritual matters.

Columnist Mitch Albom wrote a book about his weekly conversations with Morrie Schwartz a patient dying from ALS. Schwartz said he felt that facing death was a wake-up call leading to an enhanced ability to see more clearly life's real priorities.

Like most of us, Morrie wanted to die serenely, not in a state of fright. He wanted to know what was happening to him, to accept it, to get to a peaceful place and let go. To do so he used meditation.

VII. The Dying Process

Chapter 2 Death and Dying

As noted, the Dying Process is a rite of passage for the spirit and soul to depart the earth, hopefully bound for the presence of God.

- *When you enter the last stage of your existence as a human being, your body will begin the physical process of shutting down.*

- *This is most often a somewhat orderly series of progressive physical changes that end when all your physical systems cease to function.*

- *At or near the end of this process, your spirit and your soul will seek release and begin to pull away from your body.*

- *Loved ones who are present may be able to assist this process by gently encouraging you to "Let go."*

You can expect the following physical symptoms as your body goes through the final dying process:[19]

1. **Coolness** – *Your hands, arms, feet and then legs may be increasingly cool to the touch, and the color of your skin may change with the underside of your body becoming darker as your skin becomes mottled. This is a normal indication that blood circulation is decreasing to your body's extremities. A blanket may be needed to keep your body warm.*

2. **Sleeping** – *An increasing amount of your time will be spent sleeping, and you may seem to be uncommunicative or unresponsive and at times difficult to arouse. In this situation, it is best for visitors just to sit with you and hold your hand. When talking, they should speak softly even though you may not respond. They should never assume you couldn't hear, as hearing is the last of the senses to be lost.*

3. **Disorientation** – *You may become confused about time, place and the identity of the people around you including your family and friends. Visitors should identify themselves by name, instead of assuming you will recognize them.*

4. ***Speech and sensory functions*** – *Your speech may become slurred and your vision impaired.*

5. ***Incontinence*** – *As the transitioning process continues, you may lose control of your bladder and your bowels, so you will need to be kept clean to be comfortable.*

6. ***Congestion*** – *You may have loud gurgling sounds coming from your chest, which is a normal result of secretions into your lungs. Your head should be gently turned to one side to allow drainage through your mouth.*

7. ***Restlessness*** – *You may make restless and repetitive motions such as pulling at your clothes or the bed linen. Although this may signify anxiety, it is not unusual and you should not be restrained, rather those around you can calm you by speaking in a quiet natural way, massaging your forehead and reading to you or playing soothing music.*

8. ***Fluid and Food Decrease*** – *You may experience a decrease in thirst and appetite, wanting little or no fluid or food. Small ice chips, frozen Gatorade or juice may refresh your mouth and if you are still able to swallow, fluids may be given to you in small amounts by syringe. A cool moist washcloth on the forehead may increase your physical comfort.*

9. ***Urine Decrease*** -- *Your urine output normally decreases and may become "tea colored," and you may sweat profusely.*

10. ***Breathing Pattern*** – *Your regular breathing patterns may change with variations in the pace and duration of your breaths including periods of no breathing of 5 to 30 or even 60 seconds.*

There is no death, only a change of worlds.
...Native American Chief Seattle

You may also have periods of rapid, shallow, pant-like breathing indicating a decrease in circulation to your internal organs. Hand holding and gentle support and encouragement could be helpful.

11. **Withdrawal** *– You may seem to be unresponsive, withdrawn or in a comatose state. This indicates preparation for release, a detaching from surroundings and relationships, and a beginning of "letting go."*

12. **Hearing** *-- Since **hearing** will normally remain functional all the way **to the end**, it will be important for those around you to continue to remain calm and supportive. They should speak to you in a normal tone of voice identifying themselves by name.*

13. **Decreased Socialization** *- As the end approaches, you may want to be with very few people or just one person. This can be a sign that you are preparing for release and that you feel you need their support, affirmation or permission to go.*

14. **Letting Go** *-- Dying people are often reluctant to let go because they are concerned for the welfare of those being left behind. For this reason, it can be important for loved ones to let them know it is okay to go.*

15. **Saying Goodbye** *– When you are ready to depart, and if you are able to do so, you may want to express your love for those closest to you and thank them for being part of your life.*

It is said that those with the strength and love to sit in silence with a dying human being will know that generally the moment of death is neither painful nor frightening, but a peaceful cessation of the body's functions.

**I must be willing to give up what I am
in order to become what I will be.**
...Scientist Albert Einstein

VIII. Signs of Death

- *The body you leave behind will exhibit no breathing, no heartbeat, released bowel and bladder, and it will be unresponsive with no discernible electrical activity in the brain.*

- *Your eyelids may be slightly open with your pupils enlarged, and your eyes fixed on a certain spot.*

- *Your jaw will probably be relaxed, and your mouth slightly open.*

- *The legal determination of death is often based on a lack of electrical activity in the brain, absence of breathing, no heartbeat and no response to external stimuli.*

The aftermath of a loved one's death can be a trying experience depending on how well prepared the affairs of the deceased were in advance.

The burial process and expense are likely to require several decisions that are best made well in advance... (See the following Death & Dying Pre-departure Checklist)

The legal issues involving the distribution of the deceased person's property, assets and debts can also create a great deal of difficulty if there is no will.

Families have been broken up with suspicion and bitterness over even limited belongings left when the last parent dies. Therefore, it is always best to leave a bequeath list of who might have first choice for particular items.

Often it is items of sentimental value as much as material value that can cause serious conflict among siblings.

IX. Near Death Experiences

As previously noted, researchers studying Near Death Experiences (NDEs) define them as a vivid instance where a human soul (consciousness) temporarily departs a body that is no longer showing signs of life. This may be the result of surgery, cold water drowning or other accidents after which the person is physically revived.

The experiences reported by souls while outside their bodies can shed light on the meaning of death and what may await us beyond the grave. The following are a couple of examples of NDEs reported in Professor Mark Berkson's course on Death, Dying and the Afterlife:[20]

A migrant woman named Maria suffered a heart attack in Seattle Washington. At the hospital, she was assigned a social worker named Kimberly Clark.

After surgery, Maria told Clark that she felt herself rise up well above her body during surgery to where she was able to watch the doctors working on her body below.

Maria further related that her spirit moved on outside the hospital where she noticed a tennis shoe on a 3rd floor ledge of the building with one lace lying under the heel. Hearing this, Clark went up to the third floor, and to her amazement, she saw the tennis shoe exactly as Maria described it.

Another case involved Pam Reynolds who suffered a brain aneurysm in 1991. Neurosurgeon Robert Spetzler conducted a successful hour-long operation during which time Reynolds body temperature was reduced to 60 degrees stopping her heart. Reynolds brain waves were completely flat.

Upon regaining consciousness, Reynolds reported that she had felt herself floating over her body watching the doctors use a unique bone saw to open her skull. She described the saw in perfect detail.

Surveys indicate that over the past fifty years as many as 25 million people or 3-5 percent of the global population has experienced an NDE.[21] *Dutch cardiologist Dr. Pim van Lommel in a study of revived heart attack patients discovered that 18 percent experienced an NDE.*

Dr. Bruce Greyson and other NDE researchers have identified the following seven-part pattern to many NDEs worldwide:[22]

1. *An out of body experience*
2. *The feeling of being in a tunnel*

3. *A bright light of love and acceptance*
4. *Encountering deceased loved ones or religious figures*
5. *Experiencing a sense of peace and well-being*
6. *A rapid life-review*
7. *A reluctance to return to human life*

As a result of NDEs, most people report becoming better, less selfish more thankful and happier beings who no longer fear death. However, not all NDEs are pleasant.

Noted NDE researcher P.M.H. Atwater found that of the adults she studied, fifteen percent had unpleasant hell-like NDEs, while forty-seven percent described pleasant, heaven-like experiences. The others were less specific.

Of course, there are skeptics who believe they can account for the NDEs people experience, as being a product of the biological and chemical aspects of the human brain. However, that simply cannot explain the facts that souls have observed while out of body.

X. Elizabeth Kubler-Ross on Life after Death[23]

The world's foremost researcher on death and dying, Elizabeth Kubler-Ross M.D. spent years sitting at the deathbeds of a great many elderly people and doomed children listening closely to what they had to say as they approached and experienced the end of their human lives.

She reports that she and her assistants also studied over 20,000 cases of people from all over the world who had been declared clinically dead, but who subsequently returned to life.

The near-death experiences of so many people provided fascinating insight into what we might expect during and after death. Dr. Kubler-Ross noted the following observations:

Chapter 2 Death and Dying

- *She likens the experience of human death as the occurrence of a butterfly emerging from its cocoon.*

- *As soon as a damaged and dying human body can no longer support the soul within, the soul emerges from the body.*

- *When your soul emerges from your body, you may find that you can perceive everything happening at the place of your body's death.*

- *During their out-of-body experiences, the souls report being in possession of a new and perfect human style body that is lighter than air and moved by thought.*

- *Once out of your old body, you will realize that you are no longer bound within the concepts of time or distance.*

- *When your old body dies and your soul emerges, you will be met in the new dimension of your existence by the souls who have loved you, meant the most to you and preceded you in death.*

- *After meeting your loved ones, you will transition through a tunnel or across a bridge or passage where you will be met by an awesome and brilliant white light that engulfs you with intense, unconditional love.*

- *You will come to understand that life on earth is just a school we have to pass through to learn certain lessons. When we have mastered the lessons, we can go back to our home dimension.*

- *Evidently, in the presence of the intense light, we will review our lives in detail, recalling every thought word and deed. We will make our own heaven or hell by the way we lived.*

- *You will come to realize that you were your own worst enemy as you struggled against the trials of life and the opportunities to grow.*

- *On earth, we are never given more challenges than we can bear. However, being unaware of this, some people give in too soon.*

- *Death, she says, is like moving from one house to another.*

<u>The Following are Quotes from Elisabeth Kubler-Ross:</u>

"All the challenges, trials and tribulations in life are opportunities to grow, refine and temper the mettle of your soul."

"Death is simply a shedding of the physical body like the butterfly shedding its cocoon."

"When we have passed the tests and learned that which, we are sent to earth to learn, we are allowed to graduate."

"We are allowed to shed the body that imprisons our souls."

"For me, death is a graduation."

"I say to people who care for people who are dying, if you really love that person and want to help them, be with them when their end comes close. Sit with them - you don't even have to talk. You don't have to do anything but be there for them."

"I've told my children that when I die, to release balloons in the sky to celebrate that I graduated."

"Death is the final stage of growth."

"If we could understand the state of unconditional love that has no claims or ifs, then we could all be whole and healthy, and all of us would be able to fulfill our destiny in a lifetime."

Garden Tomb of Jesus Christ in Jerusalem, Israel

XI. Death & Dying Pre-departure Checklist

If you have been identified with a terminal condition and if you still have time to take care of your affairs, the following checklist may help you identify some of the things that need to be done.

Depending on your condition, you might want to share the list with those you can trust to help you make decisions and put your affairs in order. The more you can accomplish the easier it will be on your loved ones who may be suffering and emotionally distraught at the time of your departure.

__1. Advance Medical Directive / Living Will__ - Be certain to have in writing the extent of medical care you wish to have when you are dying, and make sure a copy of the form is in your medical record and that your Medical Power of Attorney has a copy.

__2. Medical Power of Attorney__ - Complete a Medical Power of Attorney form to identify in writing the person you want to make any critical medical decisions for you if you become unable to communicate. Name an alternate in case the primary person is unavailable, and let both know your preferences.

Many States have developed forms that combine the intent of the durable power of attorney (to have an advocate) and the intent of the living will (to state choices for treatment at the end of life). Each State regulates advance directives differently, so you may need to consult with the physician, nurse, social worker or family lawyer.

__Ethical Will__ - You can assemble an informal ethical will with such information as follows:

1. *You can explain where you would prefer to die: at home, in a hospice, a hospital, nursing home or elsewhere for it will become your portal to the next world.*

2. *You might want to consider resolving any existing disputes with family or others.*

3. *You might want to designate people you would most like to have present and holding your hands when you die.*

4. *You may request certain music, poems, prayers, etc. at or near the time of your death.*

5. *You might want to have a particular pastor, priest or other religious representative present.*

6. *You may want to explain the kind of funeral service or memorial service you might prefer.*

7. *You should indicate your preference for the disposal of your body: burial or cremation.*

8. *You should leave instructions for the disposition of your cremated remains or a location for burial of your body.*

Financial Will

9. *You should have a legally binding will to designate the people you want to receive your financial assets and your worldly possessions, and designate an executor.*

10. *If appropriate, you should designate who you would prefer to have raising children or taking care of pets.*

11. *You should make sure people are aware of any life insurance policies you may have.*

12. *Someone should be made aware of safe deposit boxes, their contents and the location of the keys.*

13. *Someone needs to know if you have burial allowances, veterans benefits etc.*

14. *You should make known any debts you owe or financial obligations you may have.*

15. *You should make known any income payments you receive that will need to be terminated at your death.*

16. *Make sure information like the following is updated and available:*

   - *Your Full legal name and residence*

- *Birth date and place*
- *Social Security number*
- *Major employer(s) and dates of employment*
- *Education and military records*
- *Sources of income and assets; investment income (stocks, bonds, property)*
- *Insurance policies, bank accounts, deeds, investments, and other valuables*
- *Most recent income tax return*
- *Money owed, to whom, and when payments are due*
- *Credit card and charge account names and numbers*

Spiritual Affairs

17. At this point getting right with God should be your highest priority.

18. Seek forgiveness for the errors you may have made in living.

19. Consider the salvation of your soul.

Other Concerns

20. Utility, cable, phone and mail service may need to be discontinued.

21. An obituary will need to be composed.

22. You might want to compose the inscription for your tombstone. Ruth Graham copied hers from a road sign that read: "End of construction. Thank you for your patience."

23. Check with funeral homes to see what literature and pre-arrangements are available.

"Death and love are the two wings that bear the good man to heaven."
...Famed Renaissance artist Michelangelo

XII. Summary

All human beings go through the experience of death, usually as a result of the body's physical aging process.

- *Dying is the process of transitioning from the land of the dying to the land of the living, from this dimension to the next.*

- *It is the event that will mark the end of your opportunity as a human being to improve your soul, to find a meaningful way to contribute to society and to find a meaningful relationship with the Divine.*

- *Death is a rest from the trials and exertions of this life.*

- *Since hundreds of millions of other people have made it through the conversion experience we call dying, there is no reason you cannot do so as well.*

- *"Dying well" means going out full of faith and confidence that by the grace of God you are graduating to a better dimension.*

- *Dying well also means caring about those caring for you by being the most pleasant and cooperative patient you can be.*

- *Make sure you are ready by using the Pre-Departure Checklist.*

- *By all means do whatever you need to do to get right with your maker while there is still time.*

- *Death is the door at the end of this fantastic pilgrimage that has given us the opportunity to prepare our souls with virtue, faith and courage for the next event on the other side of death's door.*

- *Death can be intimidating even when you know that to be absent from the body is to be present with the lord, but fear not as you become a veteran of the great tests of human life.*

The day of death is better than the day of birth.
...Ecclesiastes 7:1

Another soul wings its way to heaven.

The following thoughts are from an 1805 sermon
on the Infirmities and Comforts of Old Age
by Joseph Lathrop (1731-1820).

As we come into this world, so we depart, physically impotent, feeble and helpless. This state of infirmity and anxiety, painful in itself, is rendered more so by the recollection of what we once were and by the uncertainty of what we shall soon become.

As our physical man deteriorates, we must learn to depend more and more on God's grace to strengthen the inward man in preparation for what draws nigh. In our increasing infirmities, we should perfect our prayers with a strengthening soul until at last we can stand calmly on the brink of eternity.

The twilight years of our physical decline are but a moment in eternal time to prepare us for a closer glory with divine Providence. We should apply ourselves in prayer for the grace to bear our troubles with fortitude and virtue and to meet death with dignity and courage.

The elderly human, taken off by his infirmities from the active business of life, can in no way do more service for God and mankind, than by demonstrating a visible example of spirituality, faith and hope, in the face of his approaching demise.

To have the comfort of faith when you need it most, you must develop it beforehand by study, contemplation, prayer and the exercise of devotion to holy sacraments. Thus, you should cultivate the spiritual temper of faith early for it may be no easy matter to take it up in the waning days of your physical being unless you are accustomed to it beforehand.

Embrace faith in your soul, cultivate the holy mindset it requires; maintain the good works it enjoins, and ascertain your title to the eternal blessings which it proposes. Thus, lay up for yourself a good foundation of belief against the time to come when your soul alone will face the great abyss between this life and the next.

The day after the seminar, our Socialist overlords tell us that if we cooperate and start filling out the required health assessments on our older retired patients, they will release a vanload of the medical supplies and food being sent to us by Doc's friends and former patients in other countries.

Doc tells them we will complete the forms. However, he tells us to fill out the forms as if everyone is healthy. It will probably take a while for their bureaucrats to notice what we are doing. The next day the van arrives with the desperately needed food and medical supplies.

Our archeologist friend Dr. Jones sent an email telling Doc that many non-socialist countries are now offering U.S. medical personnel and scientists free moving expenses, big bonuses and terrific pay and benefit packages plus freedom from Socialism to move to their countries.

There are now over 50 thousand vacancies for nurses at U.S. hospitals and many are closing due to a lack of medical professionals.

Every human life ends the same way. It is only the details of how we live and how we die that distinguish one of us from another.
...Author Ernest Hemingway

Chapter 2 Death and Dying

San Marino 10 lire coin year 2000

After all is said and done, death may be simply the ultimate healing.

Question: *The famous Russian author Leo Tolstoy lamented in his book "A Confession": What will become of my life? Is there any meaning in my life that the inevitable death awaiting me does not destroy?*

Answer: *His soul and its fitness for holiness (or not) is the meaning in his life that the inevitable death awaiting him cannot destroy.*

**I entered and beheld with the eye of my soul...
The Light Unchangeable.**
...St. Augustine

---

[1] J.P. Moreland, *The Soul: How We Know It's Real:* Chicago: Moody, 2014 p.138

[2] Professor Mark Berkson, *Death, Dying, and the Afterlife*, Course Guidebook, The Teaching Co., Chantilly, VA, 2016, p.5

[3] Bob Welch, *52 Lessons from A Christmas Carol,* Thomas Nelson, Nashville, 2015 p.100

---

[4] Professor Daniel Breyer, *The Dark Side of Human Nature,* The Teaching Company, Chantilly VA. 2019 course guidebook p.63

[5] Ibid

[6] National Vital Statistics Report, Volume 53, Number 5 (October 2004) Causes of Death, USA, 2002.

[7] www.benbest.com/lifeext/causes.html September 8, 2006.

[8] National Geographic Magazine, 2006 likely between June and November. On an unnumbered page titled Geography.

[9] Ibid

[10] National Vital Statistics Report, Volume 50. Number 15 (Sept. 2002) Causes of Accidental Death, USA

[11] Bottom Line Personal newsletter, August 15, p13.

[12] National Geographic Magazine, 2006 likely between June and November. On an unnumbered page titled Geography.

[13] Professor Mark Berkson, *Death, Dying, and the Afterlife*, Course Guidebook, The Teaching Co., Chantilly, VA, 2016, p.22

[14] Elizabeth Kubler-Ross, *On Death and Dying*, Celestial Arts p235

[15] Dunn, Hank. *Hard Choices for Loving People*. A&A Publishers, Herndon VA.

[16] Billy Graham, *Nearing Home* (Nashville: Thomas Nelson, 2011), ix

[17] Ibid, p118

[18] Norman Vincent Peale, *Seeds of Faith*, Ideals Publications, p13, Nashville, 2004

[19] Elisabeth Kubler-Ross, *On Death and Dying*, Celestial Arts p246.

[20] Professor Mark Berkson, *Death, Dying, and the Afterlife*, Course Guidebook, The Teaching Co., Chantilly, VA, 2016, p.178

[21] Ibid p.180

[22] Ibid p.180

[23] Elisabeth Kubler-Ross, *On Death and Dying*, Celestial Arts p246

Chapter 3

<u>Conclusion</u>

Hello good reader, I am the Colonel, and I am honored to guide you through the conclusion of our book where we will review important tenets of faith and the meaning of human life and its demise, and together we will come face to face with death itself.

First an update on our country's disastrous experience with Socialism. The presidential elections have finally arrived, and everyone believes the Socialist regime will be soundly defeated in the congress and for the presidency. However, the administration is now saying there were irregularities in the voting and electronic interference in the vote by foreign powers opposed to Socialism. We are told by the fake news media that it will take time for the administration to purge the irregularities and get an accurate vote count. Yeah right! We'll see about that.

In the meantime, I am going to try to bring you with me through the dying process as I go hopefully to meet my maker. I trust I have lived this life well enough to successfully transition my soul into the higher spiritual dimension through that creepy route we call death.

I have tried to deny death is here, but I finally realize there is no way out. Incapacitated on my deathbed, I am asking Carter and Warden to read the summary of our Handbook of the Soul because I do not want us ever to forget what we worked so hard to learn.

We live better when we remember we will die.
...Unknown

The Meaning of Death

The boys by turn are reading a summary review of our Handbook of the Soul as follows:

1. *There is one God of Divine goodness with Whom souls may exist in a heavenly dimension.*

2. *The heavenly dimension must be vast and based on consciousness and spirit. Every inch of it must be infused with the spirit of God, and it is probably our natural home dimension.*

3. *Thinking that the visible dimension of our earthly existence is all that exists is like being shut in a small closet and believing it is all that exists because it is all we can see and touch.*

4. *Human life should be a journey from darkness to light, ignorance to wisdom and from selfishness to love and compassion.*

5. *Human Life on earth may be a little like a challenging adventure-reality course where we are given a chance to develop spiritual strength and virtuous character by properly overcoming the challenges and difficulties we must face.*

6. *The **meaning** of life is the opportunity it provides to develop a more **virtuous character** that can create a change in our souls to bring us closer to God.*

7. *The **purpose** of this life is to make holy our **relationship to God** by living in right **relationship to him and by living in a right, unselfish relationship with other people**.*

I am getting cold and weak and it's hard to stay awake. I need to rest a little before going on. At age 84, I know I am very close to the end of my journey on earth, but I very much want to remind my family of what we learned about the true existence of human beings as eternal souls.

I am OK now boys, please resume the review.

"Time is a great teacher; unfortunately, it kills all its pupils."
...Hector Berlioz

Chapter Three

8. *Each human is a **spirit** and a **soul** with many capacities combined into faculties of mind, will and emotions. The soul has many properties such as conscience, character, consciousness and transcendence.*

9. *We are **not** just **helpless** victims of fate experiencing the aimless unfolding of meaningless lives. We are very **powerful, eternal spirits** with souls directing our energy to making our lives as meaningful as possible by developing virtuous, godly character.*

10. *We have a moral duty to work hard to **develop virtue** and **overcome selfishness**. We must be team players helping as many other people as possible to progress along their journeys of life.*

11. *Learning to **unselfishly** carry out our human **roles** and our **responsibilities** to our families and to other people, gives **social** and **moral purpose** and **meaning** to our lives.*

12. *We are faced with a lifetime of challenges not of our making **that are making us** by the way we respond to them. In addition, we can cause our own problems or opportunities by the **thoughts** we think, the **choices** we make, the **actions** we take and the **friends** we make.*

13. *The following twenty-two very important eternal values form the **basis of good character** and are often overlooked or disregarded in contemporary culture.*

1. Truth	12. Wisdom
2. Honor	13. Moderation
3. Dedication	14. Faith
4. Unselfishness	15. Hope
5. Generosity	16. Love
6. Virtue	17. Patience
7. Freedom	18. Optimism
8. Respect	19. Humility
9. Justice	20. Forgiveness
10. Temperance	21. Compassion
11. Courage	22. Prudence

We need to stop again; my mouth is so dry; will someone please get me some ice? Thanks, that really helps. I am getting very tired now....

The Meaning of Death

My eyelids are opening so slowly, and why is everything so dim? I feel disoriented.......Uh, but I'm OK; was I out for long? About thirty minutes you say, well, I'm sorry, boys please read on.

14. *A respect for the power of God is deep within every human spirit, but in this confusing dimension, it requires a self-conscious act of faith to acknowledge God's existence.*

    - *In this realm, consciously giving one's self the consent to seek, search and pay attention to the existence of the force of supreme good is the way open to human beings to escape the bondage of physical needs.*

    - *The link from the praying human soul to the transcendent power of God is a path of saving grace available to every human being.*

15. *There are at least 38 virtues to aspire to, and the actual **acquisition** of a virtue is much more important than just knowledge about it.*

16. *Components of human happiness in a modern life include the following:*
    - *Adequate food*
    - *Shelter*
    - *Good relationships with other people*
    - *Physical security*
    - *Access to good health care*
    - *Educational opportunities*
    - *Opportunity for free expression of ideas*
    - *Adequate leisure time*
    - *Possibility of creative expression*
    - *Personal development and spiritual growth*

17. *The great philosopher Emanuel Kant saw life as a battle between duty and inclination. He reasoned that there must be an infinite period of time for us to reach spiritual perfection and moral purity: hence, there must be life after death.*

Chapter Three

18. *Kant also concluded that as important as reason is to human understanding of this world, human **reason is incapable** of comprehending divine truth and ultimate reality.*

19. *Individuals should have the maximum personal freedom and liberty that is consistent with the liberty of others. For this reason, we should resist the growing intrusion of government into the private sphere of individual's lives.*

20. *Even well-meaning agencies of government are inefficient by nature because the managers and employees lack any motivating incentive of profit. Socialism and Communism are the worst because they destroy all the incentives in the entire economy, eventually condemning the populace to poverty.*

I am sorry guys; I just can't stay awake. I am so tired, and my mind is drifting off somewhere again. My breathing is so slow and shallow that it's making me weak, but I just cannot draw deeper breaths. I can feel a nurse taking my pulse, and I hear her saying it won't be long now......and asleep I am again.

I hear the music I requested, and my loved ones are praying for my salvation and a painless crossing. Hey, wait I think I'm back. I am still alive! However, my voice is so weak and slurred that only my wife who is closest can hear me. Yet to me, my soul my spirit still feels as young and strong as ever. It's just that I can't get my tongue or body to move much.

Brenda, pleaseeee take my hannnd and uh... ask boysss continuuuue.

21. *The moral state of a country is a reflection of the character of the souls of its citizens combined.*

22. *If freedom from poverty is an acceptable goal, then it is virtuous to act on it for oneself and for others. The invisible hand of a free market economy allows us to help others even as we are motivated by immediate and powerful incentives for aiding ourselves and our loved ones. With Free Enterprise Capitalism, we benefit ourselves by benefitting others.*

No body gets out of this life alive.
...Author Anthony DeStefano

23. *Some of the most important things in life might not be so easy to understand in youth.*

24. *At death, we depart the land of the dying for the land of the living with hope that we have lived our lives well enough here to pass muster there.*

Uh,...Verrry goood, boysss... ttthanks you readinggss... I feel that I am withdrawing, losing touch and starting to gather my spirit and soul within. Matt, Casey, Carter and Warden have taken my other arm, I am thinking what a privilege it has been to live with you all. I cannot speak, but know that I love you and wish you God speed through the rest of your journeys; keep the faith and surely, I will meet you on the other side.

My eyes are losing focus; It's getting dark, I can't see! I can't see anything! I can't even hear now. I am feeling deeply isolated. Now, a series of shuddering and a growing vibration deep within as if I am moving inside myself.

My soul is shaking away from my faithful old body. Uumph,.....Ooaaoah....aaaaarrrgh....Oh, and yes, I'm out!...spinning, slowing, trying to get oriented, trying to stand vertically, but doing better laying in the air face down so free and buoyant! Yahoo, I'm speeding about at the wisp of a thought!

I am so light and fast; it's just amazing! Yet, peering down, I can see that you are all looking sad. Please don't cry. If only you could see me zipping around above you and darting about like a humming bird. Now this spiritual agility is really, really cool.

What? Uh oh, now I'm being pulled away against my will toward some kind of cloud bank...Goodbye my earthly family, and to you good reader for your attention. My faith and my character now determine my fate.

"To be absent from the body is to be present with the Lord." Sure enough, I made it straight to heaven where I am present with the lord. When I arrived here my mind expanded and was filled with spiritual perception.

I am allowed now to try to send one message to humanity. I am told that most messages never get through to Human beings on earth because most humans are not spiritually minded enough to perceive them.

I am going to try to get it through to the spiritually attuned mind of "Doc" Moses when he prays. That critical message, as follows, is to explain human salvation through the sacrifice of Christ Jesus and why you must believe in him (or be perfect) to ever become **present with God in heaven**.

<u>Handbook of the Soul</u>

Conclusion

The Meaning of Death

Spiritual message
From the Colonel
Heaven
00/00/00

*When we understand the process of the transformation of our spirit and soul, we will better accept life's challenges and difficulties knowing that **only by living properly through them** can we gain spiritual strength, maturity and peace and eventually liberation from our earthly bodies.*

The Human Tragedy of Sin

1. *Sin is the result of desire, the human desire to take God's place and become the center and measure of all things and to "know" (decide) for themselves what is good and what is evil (Gen. 3:4-5). Titus 3:3-7 says people in their natural state are foolish, disobedient, deceived and enslaved to various lusts and desires. Nevertheless, they consider themselves to be "basically good".*

2. *Sin is rebellious behavior that God has forbidden in humans (for their own good). So, when they rebel and commit sin anyhow, it is a huge, spiritually hateful, grave, deadly and rebellious insult thrown right straight in the face of the God who made them and loves them.*

3. *In the human race, sin is **all-pervasive**. Every aspect of human existence is affected by it. Sin blinds the mind; corrupts the will and perverts the emotions causing disorder and conflict in the human personality.*

4. *Sin is **irrational** and there is no wisdom in it. Sin is **deceitful** with the victims being unaware that they're deceived.*

5. *One of the most fearful things about sin is its power to **harden** the conscience of those who practice it (Heb. 3:3). Sin seems to concern sinners less and less the further they sink into it.*

6. *Everyone who commits sin is the slave of sin" (John 8: 34).*

7. *Sin is **debasing and defiling;** it turned angels into demons and it turns good people into spiritually irrational animals.*

8. *Genesis 4:8 tells us that Cain, the first human child ever born, killed his only brother Abel.*

9. *Humans have a **corrupt soul** for as Jesus says in Mark 7:20-23: Out of the soul of humanity proceed evil thoughts, fornications, thefts, murders, adulteries, deeds of coveting and wickedness, as well as greed, malice, deceit, lewdness, sensuality, envy, slander, pride, arrogance and foolishness. People defile themselves when from within their souls, come forth these evils.*
10. *We also have a "**bad record**" because we all have a life-long "rap sheet" of sins already committed against God, for which fair, holy justice demands an appropriate penalty be paid.*

Guilty Humanity, a Righteous God and Justification

1. *Most humans, deep down, feel outrage when an obvious injustice takes place, which is a reflection of God's just nature in their souls.*
2. *There is no way completely just, honest and righteous **judges** could ever release absolutely guilty and condemned criminals without violating their own judicial duty, their principles, their character, self-respect and their reputations by accepting a bribe or engaging in other dishonesty which truly honest judges could not do.*
3. *So, then God, the very essence and basis of all justice, cannot **judge sinful humanity** as innocent without becoming a disgrace to Himself and violating His own character which He cannot do.*
4. *However, God loves you and dearly wants you to be innocent and holy enough to abide with Him in eternity. But He cannot just sweep human sins under the rug, because sin, doing what God has forbidden, is a grave and rebellious insult to God. And sinful humanity cannot exist spiritually in proximity to a pure and holy God. There is but one solution to this dilemma: "**Imputation**".*
5. *Imputation is similar to you wrecking your father's car but your older brother, in the car with you, says he was the one driving. The responsibility is imputed to your brother who takes the punishment in your place.*
6. *Or Imputation is something like you being arrested for driving way too fast through town. The judge says you must pay a fine of $1000 and you will be jailed until you do. However, you don't have the*

money. But your father loves you and wants you home and out of jail, so he asks your wealthy big brother to pay your $1000 fine. So, the penalty is moved over to your big brother who can and will pay the fine to get you out of jail.

7. So, imputation of sin is where someone else assumes a sinner's guilt and pays the penalty for it. Sin must be satisfied by each sinner's own suffering forever, or it must be satisfied by someone else suffering greatly on the sinners' behalf.

8. To compensate for all the sins of all humanity, past, present and future, that someone else must be very, very worthy and capable of extreme suffering. Like a prisoner swap in times of war, one side might exchange one valuable, high ranking, captured enemy general to get back a thousand of their regular soldiers.

9. But who, therefore, is valuable enough and capable of suffering intensely enough to become the acceptable punishment for all humanity's spiritually costly sins? And who in all creation could possibly care enough about Human beings to be willing to pay such an appallingly high and dreadful price?

10. To humanity's **very great good fortune**, the only being in creation capable of doing so has volunteered to do just that. To take your eternal spiritual punishment for you. Your sins are no longer attributed to you, because they have been **imputed to Christ**, who accepted them as if they were His own sins, and He suffered immensely to pay the terrible price of all our sins in full!

11. On the scales of God's justice, the innocent blood of Christ carries so much weight that it can balance out all the past present and future sins of mankind. That is why it took the son of God to pay for all human sins because his innocent blood is worth all the millions of gallons of guilty human blood.

12. So, a substitute has suffered and died in your place! Out of everlasting love, God and his son have caused (imputed) all of your sins to fall on Jesus. Thus, they made a way to save you from spiritual justice - without God becoming an unjust judge which He could not have done.

13. *The result of the imputation of your sins to Christ is termed* **"Justification"** *because it can justify your existence in heaven.*

Justice for Jesus

14. *But how, you might ask, was it justice for Jesus? For the one who never sinned to be sacrificed for the sins of all human beings? The key is that Christ was not forced to do so, he volunteered to follow the will of his father. Nevertheless, it was an extreme sacrifice born of extreme love.*

15. *It hurt Jesus far beyond just the physical brutality, for on the cross he became* **sin itself***, therefore, becoming the focus of his Father's intense hatred for sin, which is spiritually at war with God and all he stands for.*

16. *Sin infected humanity, turning mankind, God's beloved creation, against him. To save us he had to ask the Son he loved dearly to suffer severely. Thus, did God take out all his wrath on his cherished son who on the cross became sin with all of human sin imputed to him.*

17. *It's no wonder that Jesus on the cross cried out "My God why hast thou forsaken me?" For in that moment of time, he hung murdered on the cross by men who hated him, suspended between heaven who, hated him (as human sin) and those in hell who always hated him.*

18. *Seeing the darkened heavens over Jesus as if it were closed against his cry and himself hanging between both earth and heaven as if rejected by each and to realize that all this is because of our sins, is to see clearly the holy justice and wrath of God against sin.*

19. *No one knows the depth of spiritual agony; the evil and devastation Jesus must have suffered while in hell until his father's wrath at our sin was fully spent on him.*

20. *The* **only justice for Christ** *that makes his sacrifice worthwhile is the* **faith, love and honor from those humans** *who recognize him as their savior. Those who choose not to honor such a sacrifice, do not deserve its benefits, and they are destined to pay for their own sins.*

21. *By imputing all human sin to Christ, God made a way to save you from the demands of His justice. As previously noted, this spiritual miracle is known as justification.*

22. *Through this spiritual miracle of Justification, your new status in God's eyes changes from condemned to innocent. This process of removing the sin and guilt from your name in God's record, safely **justifies** your eternal spiritual existence in heaven.*

23. *You can now be in a right relationship with God, but **only** by **believing** in the life, death and resurrection of Jesus Christ on your behalf.*

24. *For humanity, this miracle is free, though it was extremely costly for Jesus. To **accept it,** you have only to **recognize, love** and **honor** Jesus for making the spiritual sacrifice that frees you from the penalty for sin.*

Regeneration

25. *When a person becomes a Christian, they are immediately indwelt by the Holy Spirit. The Holy Spirit then brings about a spiritually new birth for their soul, regenerating it from a soul with a sin nature to a soul with a grace nature.*

26. *However, an element of the sinful nature remains as long as this body inhabits the earth. It is known as the "flesh" because it is associated with the body, and it constantly **contends** with the grace nature for control of our souls, which can result in some sinful activity.*

27. *This change in the predominate nature of our souls is termed "**Regeneration,**" and we do not feel it happening. The evidence of it is found in our changed behavior.*

28. *The act of regeneration also begins our soul's **lifelong process** of "**sanctification**", in which our souls and the Holy Spirit continue to **increase** the **holiness** of our regenerated souls.*

29. *In conclusion, **Jesus** comes to save **us** from both the penalty and the power of sin. He saved us from sin's **penalty** by imputation and justification, but by **regeneration** and **sanctification** He (through the Holy Spirit) **saves** us from **sin's power** to lead us to hell.*

Chapter Three

30. *Justification takes place in the "courtroom of God" in heaven. Regeneration and sanctification, however, must take place on earth in the soul of each Human being.*

If this message gets through, I hope it will clarify a few things about the critical role Jesus Christ plays in cosmic justice and the necessity of believing in him for the salvation of your soul.

From heaven with love,
The Colonel

Set forth below is the answer to the last of the most important and enduring spiritual questions of concern to human beings. This might be the most intriguing question of all time.

WHAT IS THE MEANING OF DEATH?

The meaning of Death is simply that we are graduating from this life and transitioning to our next dimension. It is just a portal from this world to the next. It means we don't have to live here forever.

Death adds value to life because in life's brief time-span each remaining day becomes more precious.

Death is also the ultimate deadline. For some people, death's approach gradually provides motivation and a growing sense of urgency to determine what is important in life and a limited time frame for acting on it.

We have a limited time also in which to achieve a virtuous character of personal excellence. Realizing our lives have a finish line sealing our fate should help motivate us to become the souls we need to be.

We will pursue entry to heaven when our soul's faith, character and quality are virtuous and gracious enough to enable us to fit in and thrive in an altogether positive spiritual dimension. Otherwise, there are likely alternative dimensions.

"Those things that hurt, instruct"
...Benjamin Franklin

The Meaning of Death

I am standing on the docks. A great sailing ship at my
side spreads her white sails to the morning breeze
and starts for the blue ocean. She is an object of
beauty and strength. I stand and watch her until
at length she hangs like a speck of white cloud
where the sea and sky mingle.
Then someone says:
"There, she is gone!"
"Gone where?"

Gone from my sight. That is all. She is just as large
in mast, hull and spar as she was when she left
my side and she is just as able to bear the load of
living freight to her destined port.

Her diminished size is in me, not in her.
And just at that moment when someone said:
"There, she is gone!" There were other eyes watching
her coming, and voices taking up the
glad shout:" Here she comes!"

And that ... is dying…

Henry Van Dyke

THUS, CONCLUDES

THE HANDBOOK OF THE HUMAN SOUL.

Ω

Chapter Three

The Socialist administration and their media allies are trying to convince the nation that they actually won reelection by a large margin, now that they have "adjusted" for the "voting irregularities" and the "foreign meddling".

The people know better, and we refuse to accept it. Massive strikes and demonstrations are spreading around the country with the resistance radio stations keeping the citizenry informed. Most of the police are now staying home along with sanitation, transportation and utility workers plus half the employees in the commercial and industrial workforce. Garbage is piling up everywhere and the stench they say is awful. A grim gridlock grips the nation while the Socialist try to wait it out.

Meanwhile, led by elements of APOLLYON and other radical socialists and anarchist gangs the criminals with guns are roaming the streets looting, robbing and raping at will in the name of social justice. People whose guns were confiscated are unable to defend themselves or their property, because now, predictably the only ones with guns are the criminals.

Mobs are burning and looting stores, homes and businesses and pulling down statues to the national heroes of old. The dead bodies of former property owners ravaged by dogs and birds litter the streets of big cities and the suburbs. The chaos has reigned now for over three weeks. Yet, the Socialist administration still refuses to admit defeat.

Finally, today the radio says the military has stepped in to restore order. They say they will operate the government until they can set up new supervised elections in 90 days using paper ballots to prevent fraud. The strikes are over and everyone is now focused on the upcoming elections.

Pandemonium has broken out across the nation at the announcement that the Socialists have been soundly defeated in the new elections. People are rejoicing in the streets singing, dancing and partying across the country. The national nightmare is finally over and the country has turned from Socialism back to its original values of Freedom, Democracy and Free Enterprise Capitalism.

The Meaning of Death

Although the economy is a wreck, with Capitalism's powerful incentives for investment, hard work and individual initiative restored, we have at last started down the road back to prosperity. Woe be it to anyone else that proposes Socialism for this country. If the military had not stepped in, we may have been unable to save this great nation of hope and freedom for future generations.

On behalf of our entire cast of characters, I wish you Godspeed on the rest of your life's journey, and we hope you have enjoyed and benefitted from our time together.

Our priorities shift according to life's pressures.
Faith requires constant reminders and renewals to remain strong.

When you complete this journey, you will be different from the soul that
started it. That change is what human life is about. Therefore,
try hard to become a soul that is better, not worse!

No matter how many people say wrong is right
and dark is light, it will never make it so.
... Educator Booker T. Washington

Chapter 4

Frequently Asked Questions

1. I want to believe in God, but I can't quite find enough proof that He exists, so what can I do?

As noted in the discussions of free will, there is no absolute scientific type proof of God's existence, and this is likely to be for a very good reason. However, there is a great deal of circumstantial evidence that God exists in the wonder, order and beauty of life and all creation.

Nevertheless, it may require you to make a "leap of faith" decision. You have the choice of believing that all of creation is either

- Solely the result of cosmic explosions and other unexplained forces

- The result of the work of a divine intelligence

There is a historical circumstance that has helped many to faith. It was noted by British Professor C.S. Lewis, once a confirmed atheist, who pointed out that the eleven apostles of Jesus; Peter, John, James, etc. were scared, cowed rabbits upon the arrest and crucifixion of their leader Jesus Crist with Peter even denying three times that he knew him.

However, something extremely powerful must have happened to cause a change of heart in them sufficient to motivate them to go about preaching the forbidden message of Jesus in spite of the clear threat to their lives for doing so. They were imprisoned, tortured, and eventually crucified, or beheaded for continuing to preach the divinity of Christ and their belief in him.

They were reportedly indwelt by the holy spirit and met Jesus alive following his crucifixion. It would have taken that kind of supernatural occurrence to convert those frightened apostles to such courageous martyrdom, which is a historical fact that does bears witness to Divinity.

There is no proof that God didn't use cosmic explosions to create the earth and he may have used evolution to evolve some of the current plants and other animals while creating mankind from his own image. Ultimately, you could explore the issues and study them well enough to use a combination of reason and faith to inform your own opinion.

You can review the evidence presented at the end of Chapter 1 of Book 1 then consider Pascal's Wager. As previously noted, Pascal's Wager is a simple proposition attributed to the famous French Philosopher Blaise Pascal in which he points out:

1. If you believe in God, but God does not exist; when you die you are no worse off for having believed.

2. However, if you deny God, and he does exist; you may be much worse off after death for having denied Him, having refused His grace and possibly ending up in some kind of hell.

Obviously the first option is far less risky than the second. The journey to faith is not necessarily easy, but those who truly work at it usually find it. In addition, see the answer to question 7 below.

About faith and reason Abraham Lincoln said, "I believe the Bible is the best gift God has given to man…. but for the Bible, we could not know right from wrong…take all you can from it upon **reason**, and the balance on **faith**, and you will live and die a happier man."

He who deliberately offends God does not comprehend reality.

- Some say it is necessary first to believe with faith, and, in turn, that will help you to understand with reason. Make a faith-based decision that you are going to believe in God, and begin acting on that decision with daily reading of scripture and prayer. Prayer is the beginning act of faith. It has been said that faith is the grey dawn, which proceeds the full and perfect day of knowledge.

- After praying for several months for God's divine and forgiving grace, you may begin to notice a calming reduction of apprehension, anxiety or angst in your life. This may give you an additional sign of God's existence.

- In addition, some of the things you pray for will begin to come about over time.

- These answers to prayer will of course come about in natural ways that might lead you to think it was going to happen anyhow, and that is likely to be what those without faith will tell you.

- The stronger your faith becomes, the more you can accomplish through prayer. Keep in mind that God's four answers to prayer can be yes, no, not yet or there is a better way.

2. If there is a God, why does He allow so much evil, hardship and tragedy in the world?

Many of the hardships and challenges are likely the necessary tests we must pass to develop our character, while others are due to our own poor choices. Some hardship and evil are caused by the choices and actions of other humans that impact our lives.

Part of the answer to this question is that if free will is to be preserved to allow for human spiritual development, then we must be able to experience the consequences of our actions be they good, bad or even evil. However, God hates sin and evil and is not its cause. He only tolerates it in those who insist on choosing it.

A unique feature of earthly society is that it is a place where good and evil mix freely although, there is more good than evil. However, evil is allowed to gain influence, and it is even allowed to gain the upper hand at times (Hitler, Stalin etc.) as a necessary consequence of giving free will to human beings.

- God would have to adjust reality everywhere, every second to try to keep any of the harmful effects of ill-intended human activity from bringing harm to others.

- Being God, He could do it, except that it would make bad actions less bad if they never hurt other people.

- We must learn to focus on helping and not hurting others, and we could not understand this if our actions were never allowed to hurt others such that we can see the full consequences of some of our corrupt and selfish actions.

- The sufferings of life can be understood as corrective experiences to be overcome and so utilized in the development of character in the spirit and soul.

- Perhaps there is also some tough love at work where God allows us to suffer now for a much greater good that we cannot presently foresee.

- Good parents know that there are some lessons their children will learn only the hard way. It is also necessary to feel the bad in order to appreciate fully the good in life.

God can be the toughest coach in world, if you ask him to improve your capacity for virtue, to do so he may increase your challenges. Because like athletes we increase capacity with practice.[1] Life is a chance to increase virtue via practice in tough times with tough challenges.

According to James Allen, the difficulties of life are great, its battle fierce and clarity uncertain, so much so that every hour men and women are breaking down under the strain.

However, for those who learn to fight bravely and not yield to doubt, there is certain victory ahead.[2]

"The true value of a human being is determined primarily by the measure and the sense in which he or she has attained liberation from the self."
...Genius Physicist Albert Einstein

In addition, we must allow for the fact that the reasons for the death and hardship caused by natural disasters and disease may be beyond our human comprehension, but this is no reason to blame God or doubt the existence of God.

God has created a world of human beings that are free enough even to act against his will, and possibly to go so far as to commit evil, which he hates. However, to ensure that humans are free to choose their own spiritual nature, God will tolerate evil in those that choose it. This because freedom, even if infected with potential evil, is a necessary condition for the character development required for advanced human spiritual growth.

When we realize that we are immortal souls that can be permanently harmed only by our own choices, it should give us more courage to work properly through our difficulties here on earth.

Also, when we can see that there is purpose in our challenges, it should give us reason to carry on to the best of our abilities. As previously noted, the purpose of our challenges is to grow ourselves as souls in wisdom, courage and the other virtues; to inhabit virtue and depart from vice.

Some of our greatest philosophers have concluded that while human reasoning is one of our greatest assets for understanding the world around us, it cannot be expected to explain all the logic of the world beyond us.

3. What if I believe in God, but doubt keeps creeping in?

This kind of doubt appears to be universal, so it is not unusual to have your faith in God tested by doubt. Faith is the art of holding on to what you believe in spite of the doubts that often creep into your mind. It is important to recognize that you will need to reinforce your faith through prayer and reading scriptures on a regular basis.

The act of prayer for Divine Grace is a critical step in faith; for we don't pray to a God we don't believe in or request grace and forgiveness we don't think we need. Thus, starting to pray for these things is what **positions** you to become **capable of** receiving them.

Just get the ball rolling long enough for it to become a self-reinforcing phenomenon. It takes time for your praying soul to believe enough and to become spiritually conscious enough to **begin receiving and comprehending** the free grace of God you are seeking.

- Faith is best reinforced with **daily prayer**, also religious reading or discussion and regular attendance at worship services. The more your mind is focused on your beliefs the less opportunity there is for doubt to grow.

- We have to be continuously reminded of what we believe, especially with our minds being so overexposed each day to what we don't believe.

You cannot control every thought that pops into your mind just as you cannot control every bird that flies over your head, but you can stop the birds from building a nest in your hair, and you can stop doubt from lingering in your mind.

- So just don't dwell on the doubt, use your will to push it out with positive thoughts every time it assaults your mind. "The renewing of your mind will take place little by little so don't be discouraged if progress seems slow."[3]

- Many people and circumstances in a modern society will suggest that God does not exist and that human life is meaningless. Even if you wisely choose to reject this, it will come at you time and again throughout your life.

- Knowing this, you can choose to adopt an absolute, rock bottom faith in God that you can fall back on even in your deepest levels of doubt and despair.

You just know that you know God exists, and that there is meaning and purpose in life even when you don't know or cannot remember what that meaning is or what the spiritual positions are in support of the existence of God.

We can take comfort in knowing that on earth we are in a sort of boot camp of basic spiritual training for souls. Therefore, we are being challenged to live a good and honorable life **in spite of** all of the temptation, problems and disbelief in this world.

We will pass the course by learning how to **properly inhabit our bodies** and how to develop **faith and virtue to overcome** our challenges, so that we depart earth as souls of much stronger spiritual power than we were at birth.

4. Will God keep me out of heaven if I have a poorly reformed character?

It is likely that God wants us in heaven and His grace offers everyone the chance if only they will accept it. The point is if your spiritual character is not oriented toward God, good and virtue, your **soul will not be attracted to** heaven and you may not even recognize much less accept God's grace.

Heaven can amplify, intensify and fulfill the souls of those that while on earth built a foundation of virtuous character with the faith and humility to accept God's grace. It may do nothing for those of pride and disbelief with their vices and alternate values.

Your spiritual character must be sufficiently good to be able to share in the eternal, Godly existence of love, faith and positive energy that must form the fabric of heaven.

- As Lynn observed in our story, the community of souls in heaven is likely to be composed of those who love God, care deeply about morality and goodness and who labored tirelessly on earth to develop ingrained honor and virtue.

- Self-control is the key to heaven. Use it wisely to reform your soul and heaven is yours.

- Truly, we keep ourselves out of heaven. For those who do, there are rumored to be other dimensions more suited to their souls.

Hope is most powerful when backed up by action.
...Bits & Pieces

5. What if I don't believe everything my religion teaches?

You should make every effort to pray about it, to study it thoroughly and to ask religious leaders to help you understand why it is part of the teachings of your religion.

- If you still cannot accept it, you could recognize it as something you may be too young or too inexperienced spiritually to understand and simply agree in your mind to accept the fact that now, you may not personally agree with everything taught by your religion.

- This is not unusual and you can remain faithful to everything else taught by your religion.

- If you cannot agree with most of what is taught, you may want to consider another denomination.

6. What should I do about wanting to dress immodestly to keep from looking like a prude?

It is very difficult to be modest and chaste in a society that has lost all standards of decency. The media is saturated with lewd sex from the programming to the advertisements and even the music.

People understand that sex sells, and they want to keep sexual instincts inflamed to make more money. God understands the difficulties we struggle with, but He is interested in the sincerity and the perseverance of our will to resist temptation, for it is in this crucible that good character is forged.

Even when you fail, you should pray for forgiveness and try to do better the next time. Pray about it and dress as modestly as you feel you can.

7. If I am constantly beset by fear and worry, how can I deal with it?

It is an accepted fact that it takes a certain amount of courage to exist in a world that many find to be full of anxiety and the unpredictable changes of fate that can bring suffering and sorrow in a life that is certain to end in the scary process of death.

The Meaning of Death

Don't think for a moment that you are the only one beset by fear and worry. All human beings are challenged with fear and doubt, but try to remember that your life is like that of a star actor in a play.

- The worst that can happen is that at some point you will transition from this play to the next.

- How well you carry out your roles this year helps determine your future opportunities. The best part is that you will never be given more than you could handle.

- The peace of God can surpass all such anxiety.

It is also very important to remember, "This too shall pass" and you will eventually emerge from the doubt and despair back into a happier, more balanced outlook.

- Worry and anxiety make old people out of young people.

- "Devils" exist in your fears, your doubts and your selfishness.

- The spiritual force of fear is opposite the spiritual force of faith, and it is constantly vying for access to your mind.

- Your mind is a battleground between faith and fear, honor and corruption. Think positive; reject the negative.

- Fear is negative faith — faith that something bad is going to happen.

- You are responsible for controlling your thoughts, and you can learn to do so with practice.

- You can carefully screen the information you are letting into your mind and eliminate the messages of fear and anxiety, be it the news, scary movies or violent TV shows, books, gossip, negative people or other negative input.

- In its place, you must feed your mind with mostly positive messages of hope, faith, love and happiness.

Do not be afraid of tomorrow, for God is already there.
...NVP4

- **Feed** your **faith** and **starve** your **doubts**. The contest between the good and bad within us in won by the one we feed the most. Feed faith by praying daily for Divine grace to embrace you.

Read and watch mostly positive material, develop hobbies, adopt pets, exercise and keep your mind so occupied with positive, creative, good stuff that it won't have the space or time to conjure up negative thoughts and fears.

Your mind cannot remain in a blank state; therefore, unless you control it, it will usually dwell on the nature of whatever it has been fed especially in the way of sensationalized information.

When you find your mind on fearful things, force them out with positive thoughts of good memories, faith inspiring religious verses or whatever else you want to memorize for handy mental reference.

- Say aloud the Lord's Prayer or other positive statements you have memorized for the occasion or read positive material out loud.

- Your mind cannot focus on thinking about fear and worry at the same time you are thinking positively.

- You can take control by forcing your attention on the positive until the situation passes. Review your family photo albums.

- Some people put verses from scripture with special meaning for them on post-it-notes. They stick them on the refrigerator door and refer to them whenever fear and anxiety tried to invade their minds.

- Be prepared to do so many, many times until, through repetition, over time, you establish better thought habits.

Believe that you will succeed in what you are doing, but realize that it can be a tough battle that will take time because fear, negativity and strife have become a regular part of the stressful modern diet. Don't be reluctant to get professional help from a doctor or counselor if necessary.

The Meaning of Death

- The Mayo Clinic Health Letter says to **avoid relentless negativity and complaining** because it is **draining** and **tiresome** hearing the same old gripes and negative viewpoints over and over again.

- The newsletter also councils us to find humor in things and to make our relationships with positive family and friends a priority.

According to Eleanor Roosevelt, "You gain strength, courage and confidence by every experience in which you really stop to look fear in the face. You are able to say to yourself, 'I Lived through this horror. I can take the next thing that comes along.' You must do the things you think you cannot do."[5]

Developing and sustaining faith is an ongoing process that requires time and commitment. Choosing to side with God through faith is a continual challenge. It's not something you do just once. It's an extended process of choosing to believe and act with faith over and over in every circumstance.

Ultimately, it takes faith to defeat fear, and as noted in the appendix of book three there are the following five steps to faith and dealing with doubt:

1. Make a choice, through an **act of will** to believe. It takes a serious decision to start up the road of faith for it is a long road. For most of us, it's not a simple parking spot where illumination strikes all at once. This great journey, like all others, starts with the critical first step: the **choice** to **learn to believe** in God. Throughout your life, you face the choice to believe or disbelieve.

2. Go where faith grows, where you hear it discussed and see it practiced: houses of worship, spiritual events and religious media stations. Faith increases by hearing the Word of God.

3. Read scriptures and other faith building materials. Faith comes by reading the Word of God. Regularly reading the Holy Bible is essential to building the mindset of faith. Even when the words seem to have little or

no meaning to you, they are subconsciously feeding your soul. Keep reading a page a day until you have read the bible through at least once, praying all the while to gain faith and understanding.

Don't allow your mind, accustomed only to physical facts, to oppose and crush the tender green shoots of faith as they start to emerge in your consciousness. Rather work with Divinity to absorb spiritual power and believe you are receiving it. Actively take your mind off the brake pedal of doubt and push hard the accelerator of belief to get yourself rolling. It does take **purposeful believing activity** not just a passive going through the motions. If you keep at it and stay on the runway, you will eventually take off, maybe slowly at first, but then as momentum builds, you will clear the gravitational pull of negativity and doubt and arise into the spiritual atmosphere of faith.

Keep accelerating with prayer, read the books in the bibliography of this work and others like them, watch faith-based movies, attend religious services and watch televised or video sermons and listen to faith-based radio stations and gospel or other religious music leaning ever forward into the faith you are striving for. While it may not be a short or easy route, it will be the most important one you ever travel.

Maintain your **decision** to develop faith for we can grow into it at points and times all along our lives as long as we are trying to do so. Sometimes, a life changing event such as loss of a job, divorce, a medical emergency, a close brush with death or the death of a loved one will shake up our souls enough for us to seek a better way of life. Not that such awful events occur just to bring you to faith, but they do happen and a side effect is that they can cause us to call into question the way we have been living our lives.

4. Pray for stronger and stronger faith. Make sure you are developing faith in the right things by studying the Word of God.

5. Start living like a person of faith, align your behavior more with that of faithful people. Live according to the principles and tenets of Godly conduct starting with the Ten Commandments, and pursue a virtuous character. Pray daily for God's help. Read books of prayer.

Doubt ever tries to overcome our growing faith, so expect it, and don't be troubled by it; just stay on the road and put your doubts aside. We all have doubts from time to time.

The measure of our faith is not to be found in our ability to completely avoid doubt but in our growing ability to dispel it. The stronger faith gets the easier it is to dispel doubt when it comes knocking as often it will. If it does get you down, make a comeback later.

The first steps are the hardest, because doubt and some of your own character traits will be at their strongest against you. If you push through and begin building faith it will get easier eventually. Faith is harder to gain than to sustain.

A married couple best begins the journey together for if one gets too far beyond the other, their beliefs and lifestyles begin to diverge, which weakens their relationship considerably.

As you make your way along the road toward full faith and spiritual maturity, you should be able to make more of the following improvements in your character, which will in turn continue boosting your spiritual growth creating a virtuous circle of your life:

1. *Becoming a better more respectable role model*

2. *If married, being morally pure and faithful to your spouse*

3. *Becoming more temperate in word and action*

4. *Becoming more prudent, wise and humble*

5. *Becoming more hospitable, unselfish and generous*

6. *Communicating better in a less threatening manner*

7. *Becoming sober and not addicted to substances*

8. *Becoming less self-centered and controlling*

9. *Becoming less quick tempered to anger*

You will break the worry habit the day you decide that you and God can meet and master the worst that can happen to you.
...Arnold Glasgow

10. *Becoming less argumentative, contentious or abrasive*

11. *Becoming more loving, kind and considerate*

12. *Becoming less materialistic and less concerned with possessions*

13. *Becoming better spouses and parents.*

14. *Caring more about what is good and Godly*

15. *Becoming more just, wise, discerning and fair*

16. *Becoming more self-controlled and disciplined*

8. Wouldn't it be like sticking my head in the sand to avoid the news?

No, it would be more like pulling your head out of a sandstorm of human creation designed to sell news. Remember they sell news by emphasizing and sensationalizing the worst news of the hour from every corner of the globe in almost the complete absence of good news or perspective.

- Bad news sells because it creates a fear of the bad things that might happen to us if we do not stay informed. However, thirty minutes of general news and opinion a day is usually enough keep you informed.

- An addiction to the endless flood of bad news and opinion can poison our outlook on life and sicken our spirits. Stay informed but not overwhelmed.

- Overexposure to the negativity can lead to a cynical paralysis of attitude that cuts us off from the positive creativity on which we are designed to run.

9. If Jesus died to cover our sins, what responsibility do Christians have?

Billy Graham said, "We have the responsibility to repent to God and commit to changing our lives." Change by forgoing a life of selfish pleasures and learning to live a life of righteousness.

Professor Edwin Conklin, a noted biologist, said the chance of human life originating by cosmic accident is about the same as the chance of a dictionary resulting from an explosion in a print shop.

We have the responsibility for becoming humble and spiritually hungry enough to ask in prayer to understand God's grace.

In the act of doing so, we begin the critical faith process of recognizing that God is real and that Divine grace is available to those who seek it. That is an eternally life saving step of free will on your part that only you can take.

10. How do you lean on God and give everything over to Him yet stand on your own two feet and still live a passionate, fully engaged and meaningful life?

This goes right to the heart of how to be a human by separating the physical reality we live in from the inner reality of our creative spiritual power.

The answer is to give the fear and worry about your physical existence over to God by trusting Him to make your **best** efforts good enough, while focusing your own inner creative energies on positive ways to help other people.

- Thus, you must apply yourself to providing for yourself and your family with your **best** effort without the fear and worry that only impede your progress and reduce your effectiveness. Make sure you are giving your **very best** effort, for that is what God is looking to bless.

- Learn to practice the spiritual high art of **daily prayer** in which you **request Divine grace** and thank God for it! And thank Him for seeing that your best efforts are sufficient to meet your needs by acknowledging your reliance on and trust in Him. This is a vital part of the process of aligning your spirit with the spirit of Divinity itself.

- Then ask that He guide you to your destiny as far as the ways you can best help other people through your job or by other means. It is in the fulfillment of your destiny toward others that you can learn to stand on your own two feet by rejecting pessimism and developing positive solutions with your creative energy and imagination.

Of course, you can invoke God's help whenever you need it, and if you let Him remove the roadblocks of negativity, fear and worry, you will be free to run creatively at your own speed.

11. Why pray over my food?

You ask God to bless and sanctify (sanctify means to make clean and holy) your meal to help ensure that it is fit for your consumption. Before putting anything into the body God designed, it is proper to give thanks for the nourishment and ask that it be purified for your use.

An example of such a prayer would be "Dear Lord, please bless and sanctify this food as I (we) receive it with thanksgiving. Please bless it to my (our) use and me (us) to thy service. Amen." At group meals, it is customary to have only one person pray or say grace for the meal.

12. Why is my life so full of problems when others seem to live the normal good life?

They just seem to be living the "normal good life." We are all on our best behavior when in the presence of others, and most people try to hold up the best image possible of their own situations. The "normal life" is a life of problems, difficulties and challenges mixed with pleasure, satisfaction and happiness.

How much you get of each is due in part to your development needs as a soul, your thought habits and the way you handle your challenges. It's easy to get a good grade in an **easy** course, but how much do you learn?

13. Why doesn't God make everything work out for the best in the long run?

He may very well do so, in the very long run. As for our time on earth, God helps those who with faith and courage help themselves. God wants us to succeed, but if we are to benefit, He cannot do it for us.

14. What is the difference between the purpose of my life and finding purpose in my life?

The purpose **of** your life and having purpose **in** your life are quite different considerations. As previously noted, a central purpose **of** human life is the development of your spiritual character.

Pursuing unselfish, positive activity **in** your life can be an important step in the process of your spiritual character development.

If you have no central purpose in your life, you will find yourself more vulnerable to petty worries, fears, troubles, self-pity and sickness. One of the best ways to establish a sense of purpose in your life is to find ways of helping others instead of seeking only the attainment of personal enrichment and the satisfaction of your own desires.

The question for many human beings is in what specific way can they best help other people, and how can they support themselves in the process? What if any calling has been put upon their lives, and what if any mission or causes are they destined to pursue? What exactly is their purpose **in** life?

- Some human beings develop a sense of purpose that becomes clear to them as they move toward adulthood; others develop a clearer calling at later stages of their lives.

- Still others feel a purpose, but it is somewhat vague and not easy to discern, and they must pursue it through a process of elimination or trial and error.

- Unfortunately, for some people no apparent purpose seems particularly intended for them at all. Maybe this is because they are so focused on themselves that they can discern no other direction.

- In the latter case, your ability to develop a sense of purpose and commitment from within may be an important experience necessary in the process of your spiritual development.

- In such cases, you can approach the task by gaining exposure to many sides of life through several years of academic study, travel, military service, volunteer service or various odd jobs.

Somewhere within a field of endeavor you enjoy or a related field, you should seek employment. As you become involved and more knowledgeable in a field through serious employment, your level of interest goes up, and with some positive effort you can develop a real enthusiasm to try to become the very best you can be in that line of work.

The next step in developing passion and enthusiasm for your work is to strive to become the best you can possibly be in a job, and in that way help the customers by improving the customer service and efficiency in that line of work. Another option might be to start a part time business providing a product or service that is needed in your community.

15. How can I begin to reform my thoughts?

The ways to lift your thoughts are through daily prayer, positive goals, meditation and devotion. Use persistence to keep training yourself to cast out negative thoughts as soon as they enter your mind and replace them with positive thought.

Have positive preplanned thoughts to shift to as soon as negativity enters your mind. It could be a solution to the fearful thoughts that come upon you. For instance, if you fear being lonely, imagine yourself with lots of friends.

The importance of daily bible reading, thinking about what you read and daily prayer simply cannot be over emphasized. Read a page a day starting with the new testament then the old testament until completed.

The positive preplanned thoughts could be anything positive from how much you love your children or your spouse to your favorite verses of scripture or even your hobby, your last vacation or where you would like to go on your next vacation.

- If you fear poverty, think about and dwell on how it would feel to have a great income and how you might earn it. It is not possible to hold two opposite thoughts in your mind at the same time.

When you have faults, do not fear to abandon them.
...Chinese Philosopher Confucius

- Do not think it will be easy. It may take weeks or months of continuous **thought shifting** to begin to feel progress, and of course, it will depend on how negative you are to start with.

- Avoid negative conversation and isolate yourself from negative people, negative media and other negative input, and try especially hard not to speak negativity.

- While in training, consider yourself as a soul in the intensive care unit or the recovery room of a spiritual hospital.

Your spirit is affected by the nature of your thoughts, habits and actions. Protect and regenerate your spirit, for from it **flow the forces of your existence**.

16. Why is there so much fuss over the evolution vs. creation theories? Could God have used evolution as part of his plan for the population of some of the plants and animals on earth?

Clearly God could have done whatever He chose, and there are even evolutionary interpretations of spirit as arising from the complexification of matter. Clearly, however, man was created in God's image to begin with. Unfortunately, most evolutionists believe that we all evolved from cosmic dust and primordial slime.

17. What might be the nature of hell?

Hell is certainly a separation from God. It may be a torture pit or more like a foul, corrupt and endless bog of spiritual quicksand with a slippery slope that we slide into one small selfish act at a time. "Each time we choose ourselves or our temptations over God or others…we surrender another spark of our humanity."[6]

By the time we are fully engulfed in it, we have literally dehumanized ourselves and lost all trace of human decency. By then we would rather stay in a hellish spiritual quarantine than return to God.

God surely wants all of us to progress into heaven. "On the other hand, hell seems to be something we choose by the thoughts we think, the decisions we make, the actions we take and the friends we make. No one who truly desires and seeks heaven and works hard at developing an honorable character is likely to be left out."[7]

18. If both good and bad people can be saved through faith and allowed into heaven, are the good any better off in heaven than the bad?

The question is a good one for which we, at this point, have no certain answer. If a bad person is truly saved through faith in Christ, they have become good enough at least to believe in God and accept his grace.

It is most likely that the level of virtue we attain as souls by the end of human life will affect our transition and our standing once in the next dimension. It may be that the more virtuous we are, the more fulfillment we will find in relation to Divinity in the dimension of heaven.

Although, we must be very diligent in seeking the truth that is available to us, there are things that are simply beyond our human comprehension.

19. How should I respond to people who make fun of my religious beliefs?

You will meet many people who scoff at the religious beliefs of others. Some are people with different beliefs, and some are atheists with no beliefs. This is truly a sad situation for the scoffers, as they shall someday realize.

Unfortunately, it is not uncommon, as more and more people are living a life devoid of faith. It is a sad fact that many of them are not satisfied in their own unbelief, and it galls them that others are secure in faith.

The odd thing about this is that if, after death, you find out that there is no God, you are no worse off than the atheists and maybe better off for having lived a happier more secure life. But, if they find out, after a life of disbelief, that there is a God, they may be much worse off for their lack of faith.

A true joy in life is being of use for a purpose you recognize as important, instead of being a feverish, selfish, little clod of ailments and grievances complaining that the world will not devote itself to making you happy!
... Author George Bernard Shaw

So, in the first case you have little to lose and everything to gain; whereas, they have little to gain and everything to lose. Those are bad gambling odds for any bet, much less for the bet of your eternal life. As previously noted, Jim Elliot says *He is no fool who gives what he cannot keep to gain what he cannot lose.*

20. What if I acquired addictions before I understood their negative spiritual significance, but now I find them to be very hard to defeat?

Addictions you cannot defeat with your own willpower are known as **besetting addictions**. Many young people get addicted before they realize it and usually before they are able to comprehend the extremely negative consequences of their behavior.

This alone does not make you a bad person; it may make you a good person with bad habits. However, you must continue to work very hard at overcoming the addictions, or you do risk becoming a person of bad character who has stopped trying to become more virtuous by eliminating your vices.

- For example, children are more likely to develop the bad habits of their parents if they grow up accustomed to seeing their parents drinking alcohol, using tobacco or doing drugs.

- In addition, you never know what influence you have on other people; for instance, a younger sister tells her parents that smoking can't be too bad because her older brother smokes, and we all love him and we know he's a good person.

- When you are willing to risk your children's health and future well-being, instead of doing what it takes to overcome your addictions, then you have a character problem.

- As soon as you realize you have a besetting addiction, you should get professional help to break free before it becomes more difficult.

21. What can make resolving problems between husbands and wives less difficult?

There is an old saying that "when respect goes out the window, love goes out the door" meaning it's harder to love a spouse you don't respect.

Spouses must therefore take pains to be known by their loved ones as respectable in character and appearance. Spouses must also be careful to get and stay in the habit of treating one another with respect.

In addition, men and women can handle problems in very different ways. People generally try to discover the cause of a problem and then try to figure out a way to fix or resolve it. However, women if they are troubled by a personal problem, can often cope with it by venting their feelings and "talking it out."

Very often, a woman is upset or emotionally troubled perhaps even in tears and her husband will try to help by figuring out the root of the problem and suggesting ways it could be resolved. The problem is the wife may not want to be counseled on how to "fix" it; what she often wants is consolation, commiseration and understanding.

"Talking it out" or "talking through it" means listening to the problem in all its aspects over and over in spite of suggestions about how to resolve it, which are often given the "yes dear, but yada, yada, yada" treatment instead of "oh yea, good idea, I'll try that."

Often after such a frustrating mismatch of communications, the woman will feel better and go on as if the problem has been taken care of somehow or satisfactorily addressed, and the male feels like nothing was resolved.

- But he then wonders how an issue serious enough to bring his wife to tears, can seem to evaporate into thin air when all they have done is talk about it.

- In short, men should not try to "fix" when they just need to listen.

- Women should try to acknowledge good suggestions without always trying to talk their problems completely to death without any plans to resolve the causes.

- A tradition of the Jewish people, related to this issue, is therapy of consolation known as "Sitting Sheva."

- In this tradition, a person comes and sits with a troubled friend or companion sometimes without even speaking but just "being there" listening and consoling by their presence.

In modern society, women are properly seen as equals in everything. However, much of the previously compatible cooperation among the sexes was built on different but clearer roles for each gender that may have been replaced by a competition and an unrealistic need to be independently capable of doing "it all."

- Women could get most men to do most anything for them if they just asked in the right ways.

- Women, who use the "feminine wiles" strategy of seeming to need the help of their husband's capable hands and asking in a sweet way for assistance, often find their husband's reaction to be much more cooperative.

- Women have at their disposal such power in asking nicely for help, yet some feel culturally conditioned not to use it.

22. What could God possibly want from human beings that He couldn't get more easily for Himself?

Perhaps He wants the same thing from us that we want from our children: genuine and freely given love, respect and appreciation. These are things you simply cannot force someone to give sincerely. If you create a being that cannot withhold its love from you, you don't get freely given love.

God may want a community of souls of sufficiently holy and righteous character to be able to exist undamaged in the infinitely powerful force-field of his ultra-pure, holy and sacred presence. In the extreme, radiating, spiritual energy of Divinity, souls of contaminated character with spiritually combustible material (sin) may be burned to ashes or

A harvest of peace is produced from a seed of contentment[8]

explode like popcorn in a microwave oven. Therefore, **we live this life to develop a soul of honorable character worthy of a closer relationship to God.**

23. Why would a small child or baby have to die?

The reasons for many such things are simply beyond human comprehension. There are also different ways of looking at things. For example, in Alto de Cruzerio Brazil and elsewhere in South America, a dead child is seen as an "angel baby," an innocent who will never know suffering or pain,[9] and we cannot know the particular evils from which their souls are being spared.

24. Why couldn't God have sacrificed someone besides Jesus to save us?

The principle of imputation by which all human sin, (past-present and future) is transferred to **someone else** requires that the "someone else" be spiritually strong enough to bear it, love us enough to do it and most of all - be pure, holy and innocent enough to balance out the total guilt and evil of all human sin. Apparently only His son met that full criterion.

25. What are the three critical spiritual concepts each human being must find the faith to understand and to accept?

1. First, that we are more than a physical body, indeed we are each an eternal spirit and a soul inhabiting a physical body.

2. Second, that our eternal spirits and souls were created by an eternal loving God

3. And finally, that belief in what Christ Jesus did for us is our salvation.

In this series, I have tried to address primarily the first concept by describing the nature and activity of our souls and acquainting people with them in ways that might make sense to modern human beings.

The first concept of **eternal souls** logically leads to the second concept of a **divine creator**. Once secular people see that they are living souls created by a loving God, they may find it easier to accept the case for Christian salvation.

26. Why pray for help if God already knows our need?

The fact that we pray to God reveals as much about us as it does about Him. Prayer is an important affirmation **of our faith** that God holds the answers, and that we are subject to God's will. We need God and our praying demonstrates that **we humbly realize it**.

We meet the needs of babies before they ask, but as they grow up, they are expected to ask politely for what they need or want. Some say that those who are too proud to ask don't deserve.

27. Why do bad things happen to good people?

We are all human; both the good people and the bad, therefore we are all subject to the human condition, which is a condition often subject to difficulty, physical illness, problems and evil. So, the good people aren't exempt from these things. Faith, prayer and better choices, however, can often reduce the extent of bad consequences.

28. Why couldn't we be born into heaven to begin with instead of having to first live and die on earth?

You could not have been born into heaven to start with because admission to heaven involves **a choice each soul has to make.** To qualify for heaven, you must **choose** to be **spiritually reborn** with a sincere desire to become holy enough to survive and prosper in heaven.

You must have a desire sincere enough to overcome human pride and accept through faith and humility that you **need** the saving mercy, grace and love of God. A love expressed in the sacrifice of his only Son to purchase for you a one-way ticket into the heavenly realm. A ticket you can see and hold only with faith, love, gratitude, hope and humility (holiness).

Summary

Among the important things to remember about life is that you are a spirit and soul temporarily housed in a human body for the duration of your time on earth.

- You are here in a world of good, bad and temptation to learn to exercise spiritual power to improve your quality as a soul, so that you may more successfully transition to closer harmony with God.

- Understanding is not enough. You must be able to put into practice that which you learn in the lived experience of human life.

- Your progress takes place by the virtuous changes you make in the thinking you embrace, the choices you make, the actions you take and the friends you make.

- The meaning of life is the opportunity it provides for us to improve ourselves as spirits and souls through the lived challenges of human existence.

**Whoever guards his mouth and tongue
keeps his soul from troubles.**
...Proverbs 21:23

Throughout your journey of life, it is obviously important that you look ahead in the direction you want to go and not in the opposite direction. Focus not on the ungodly, negative, evil, dark and sinful lest you end up dwelling in what you have dwelt on.
Author Jonathon Cahn in Book of Mysteries

---

[1] DeStefano, Anthony, *A Travel Guide to Life*, New York: Faith Hachette, 2014, p.237

[2] James Allen, *The Life Triumphant*, ReadaClassic.com, p.6

[3] Joyce Meyer, *Battlefield of the Mind,* Faith Words Hachette Book Group, New York, NY, 1995 p.31

[4] Norman Vincent Peale, *Seeds of Faith-Peace*, Ideals Pubs., Nashville, p. 32

[5] Eleanor Roosevelt, *You Learn by Living,* Bartlett's Familiar Quotations, *p.704*

[6] Professor Louis Markos, *C.S. Lewis* Course Guidebook, The Teaching Co.,2000, Chantilly, VA, p.17

[7] Ibid p.17

[8] Norman Vincent Peale, *Seeds of Faith-Peace*, Ideals Publications, Nashville p.20

[9] Professor Mark Berkson, *Death, Dying, and the Afterlife*, Course Guidebook, The Teaching Co., Chantilly, VA, 2016, p.40

A person's character is their fate.
...Ancient Philosopher Heraclitus

Your human soul is the essence of your being that will probably exist for eternity. As a soul, you develop the quality of your being and the course of your existence by the choices you make and your resulting conduct. If you develop properly across the arc of your existence, you may become a soul of fantastic power and ability.

Hopefully, over the course of your human life span you will learn to overcome enough temptation and sufficient challenges to leave this dimension as a soul much stronger than the possibly untested one in which you entered this earthly realm.

The awesome thing is that the choice is entirely your own for your fate is determined by the thoughts you think, the choices you make, the actions you take and the friends you make. You are yours to make or break; to win or lose; to be resolute or dissolute; and to be powerful or weak.

The ten points following are key take-aways from the series *Living as a Modern Soul in a Human Body*. Remember to choose wisely in life my fellow souls for as we choose so shall we be.

1. The meaning and purpose of human life is the opportunity it affords us to become closer to Divinity by developing more virtuous character and a robust faith in the holy Trinity.

2. We are currently souls trapped in imperfect human bodies. Our souls are composed of faculties including the mind, the will, the emotions and our eternal spirit. Each faculty contains numerous similar capacities. Joy, transcendence, consciousness, and spiritual character are a few of the properties of the soul.

I am indeed, a king, because I know how to rule myself.
...*Renaissance author & playwright Pietro Aretino*

3. Human souls and their development are based on spiritual laws and principles, and you are equipped with spiritual powers. Understanding them can help you overcome the trials and challenges of your life on earth.

4. The development of our souls takes place as we grow through challenges, successes and adversity. Only by living properly through them do we progress. Other problems and difficulties result from our poor choices and the actions of other people.

5. Evil is a result of immoral, corrupt and wicked human conduct of which God hates, but tolerates to ensure free human will, which is necessary for our spiritual development while on earth.

6. The values you hold dear and your moral and ethical conduct will help determine the character of your soul and your eternal destiny.

7. Virtues are established habits that have become character traits of a particular good behavior such as generosity or honesty. Human spiritual character traits of virtue and vice reside in the soul, and by mastering the virtues we make spiritual progress.

8. Each Human Soul should live to attain the most unselfish, positive, faith filled and virtuous character achievable, with the least amount of negativism and the fewest vices possible.

9. Through death we transition to our next dimension. Death, the ultimate deadline, adds value to life as each remaining day provides a greater incentive to align our souls with God.

10. Self-control is said to be the door to heaven. It is an important aspect of success that has no substitute, and no other power in the universe can do for us that which we must do for ourselves by entering into the practice of self-control.

The highest possible stage in moral culture is when we recognize that we ought to control our thoughts.
...unknown

"Freedom has been defined as an opportunity for self-discipline"
...34th U.S. President Dwight D. Eisenhower

I count him braver who overcomes his desires than him who conquers his enemies; for the hardest victory is over self.
...Esteemed ancient philosopher Aristotle

Author Biography

Author
James L. Cannon
Lt. Colonel U.S. Army (Ret.)

Mr. Cannon is a retired university vice president, a former economics professor and a former corporate manager.

Lt.Col. Cannon is a Vietnam War veteran, who has served in the U.S. Air Force and the U.S. Army. He was also an undercover intelligence operative and retired as a decorated Army Reserve Intelligence Officer with the Defense Intelligence Agency in Washington, D.C.

As a community leader, the author has been a successful small city mayor; a chamber of commerce president and has served on the governing boards of several public organizations.

The Colonel holds University of Virginia degrees in economics and foreign affairs; GTE marketing, management and technology degrees and is an honor graduate of the U.S. Army's Command and General Staff College and a graduate of the University of Kentucky College Business Management Institute.

The author is happily married with a beautiful wife, two children, two grandchildren, a dog and a small business. His interests include metaphysics, economics and philosophy.

The author may be contacted by email at soulsline9@gmail.com

Bibliography

  The following books have been studied in the preparation for the series *Living as a Modern Soul in a Human body*. They are recommended reading for those interested in pursuing more about the human spirit and soul in moral philosophy, metaphysics, theology and science. Thirty of the one hundred and thirty-one are highly recommended and noted with an asterisk *.

*Allen, James, *As a Man Thinketh*, New York: Penguin Group, 2008.

Allen, James, *Light on Life's Difficulties*, Blacksburg: Wilder Publications, 2008.

Allen, James, *Eight Pillars of Prosperity*, Studio City: Pacific Publishing, 2009.

Allen, James, *Above Life's Turmoil,* Lexington: WLC Books, 2009.

*Aristotle, *Nichomachean Ethics (350 BC)*, eBook, First Start Publishing, 2013.

Arntz, William, *What the Bleep Do We Know?* Deerfield Beach: Health Communications, 2005.

Baker, Goetz et al, *The Soul Hypothesis*, NY, Bloomsbury, 2013

Barnes, Bob, *Men Under Construction*, Eugene: Harvest House, 2006.

Becker, Ernest, *Escape from Evil*, New York, Free Press, 1975.

Bennett, William, T*he Book of Man*, Nashville: Thomas Nelson, 2011.

Bishop, Connie, *I Want to Teach My Child About Manners*, Cincinnati: Standard Publishing, 2005.

*Brooks, Arthur, *Gross National Happiness*, New York: Basic Books, 2008.

*Brooks, David, *The Road to Character*, New York, Random House, 2015.

Brown, D.W. *2500 Years of Wisdom*, Studio City: Divine Arts, 2013.

Browne, Sylvia*, Soul's Perfection*. Carlsbad: Hay House, 2000.

Browne, Sylvia, The Nature of Good and Evil. Carlsbad: Hay House, 2001.

Bruner, Kurt, *Inklings of God*, Grand Rapids, Zondervan, 2003.

Buckingham, Jamie, *Power for Living*. Arthur S. DeMoss Foundation, 1999.

Bunyan, John, *Pilgrim's Progress*, Chicago: Moody Bible Institute, 1960.

*Bunyan, John, Prayer, East Peoria: Versa Press, 2020

Byrne, Rhonda, *The Secret*, Hillsboro: Beyond Words, 2006.

*Cahn, Jonathan, *The Harbinger I & II,* Front Line, Lake Mary, FL, 2011.

Cahn, Jonathan, *The Book of Mysteries*, Front Line, Lake Mary, Fl, 2016.

Chesterton, G.K. *The Everlasting Man*. San Francisco: Ignatius Press, 1993.

Chopra, Deepak, *The 7 Spiritual Laws of Success*, San Rafael: NWL, 1994.

Chute, Marchette, *The Search for God*, Harrington Park NJ: R H. Sommer, 1969.

Bibliography

Chute, Marchette, *End of The Search*, Harrington Park NJ: R H. Sommer, 1947.

Cooper, John, *Body, Soul, and Life Everlasting*, Kindle Edition, 2705

Copeland, Kenneth, *Honor*, Tulsa: Harrison House, 1992.

DeStefano, Anthony, *Ten Prayers God Always Says Yes To*, New York: Doubleday, 2007.

*DeStefano, Anthony, *A Travel Guide to Life*, New York: Faith Hachette, 2014

Dickow, Gregory, *How to Hear the Voice of God* Today, Chicago: GDM, 2003

Dunn, Hank, *Hard Choices for Loving People,* Herndon: A&A Publishers, 2001

Eadie, Betty J. *Embraced by the Light*, Carson City: Gold Leaf Press, 1992

Eddy, Mary Baker, *Science and Health*, Boston, Christian Science Bd, 1934

Eldredge, John. *Wild at Heart*, Nashville: Thomas Nelson, 2001.

*Fox, Emmet. *The Ten Commandments*, New York: Harper & Row, 1953

*Fox, Emmet. *The Sermon on the Mount*, New York: Harper Collins, 1938

*Frankl, Viktor. *Man's Search for Meaning*, Boston: Beacon Press, 2006

*Freeman, W.B. *God's Little Instruction Book on Character*, Tulsa: Honor, 1996

*Getz, Gene, *The Measure of a Man*, Revell, Grand Rapids, 2016

Goetz & Taliaferro, *A Brief History of the Soul*, Wiley Blackwell, Oxford, UK

Greive, Bradley Trevor. *The Meaning of Life*, Kansas City: McMeel, 2002

*Greyson, Bruce M.D. *After (NDEs and beyond death)* NY: St. Martins, 2021

Guinness, Os. *Character Counts*, Grand Rapids: Baker Books, 1999

Habermas, Gary et al, *Beyond Death*, Eugene, Wipf and Stock, 2004

Hagin, Kenneth E. *How You Can Be Led by The Spirit of God.* Tulsa: Faith Library Publications, 1989

Hanh, Thich Nhat, Going *Home*, New York: Riverhead Books, 1999

Hays, Tommy, *First the Spirit*, Messiah-Ministries.org, 2021

Hilgert, Raymond, *Christian Ethics in the Workplace*, St. Louis: Concordia, 1984

Holmes, Andrew, *God Moments for Men*, Christian Arts Gifts, IL, 2012

Holy Bible, New King James Version, Nashville, Thomas Nelson, 1982

*Idleman, Kyle, Gods at War by, Zondervan, Grand Rapids Michigan, 2013

Jeremiah, David, *Prayer the Great Adventure,* NY: Multnomah, 1997

Jeremiah, David, *Answers about Prayer,* CA, Turning Point for God, 2022

Jeremiah, David, *Answers about Spiritual Warfare,* CA, Turning Point God, 2014

Keller, Timothy, *Making Sense of God*, New York, NY, Viking Books, 2016

*Kennedy, D. James, *Why I Believe*, Nashville: Thomas Nelson, 2005

*Kubler-Ross, Elizabeth, M.D. *On Death and Dying,* New York: Scribner-Simon & Schuster, 1997

Kubler-Ross, Elizabeth, M.D. *On Life After Death,* Berkley: Celestial Arts, 2008

Leiter, Charles, *Justification & Regeneration, Granted Ministries Press, 2009*

Lewis, C.S. *The Inspirational Writings of C.S. Lewis*, Pte Ltd, 1987

*Lewis, C.S. *Virtue and Vice*, Patricia Klein, Editor, San Francisco: Harper, 2005

Lewis, C.S. *Paved with Good Intentions*, P. S. Klein, Editor, S F, Harper, 2005

*Lewis, C.S. *The Great Divorce,* New York: Macmillan, 1952

Lewis, C.S. *Mere Christianity,* San Francisco: Harper, 1952

Bibliography

Lewis, C.S. *The Abolition of Man,* New York: Harper One, 1974

*Lindell, Mike, *What Are the Odds*, Chaska, MN: Lindell Pub. 2019

Lindsley, Art. *C. S. Lewis's Case for Christ*. Downers Grove: Inter-Varsity, 2005

Marques, Daniel, *Spiritual DNA,* Amazon.com 2017

Maxwell, John, *The Choice is Yours*, Nashville: Thomas Nelson, 2005

McFarland, Alex, *The 21Toughest Questions…*Carol Stream, IL, Tyndale, 2013

Milton & Lanzara, *Paradise Lost in Plain English,* New Arts, Belleville, NJ, 2009

Moore, Thomas, *Care of the Soul,* New York, Harper Collins,1992

*Moreland, J.P., *The Soul: How We Know It's Real:* Chicago: Moody, 2014

Moreland, J.P., *Soul & Body,* Downers Grove Il. InterVarsity Press, 2000

Murray, Andrew, *199 Treasures of Wisdom on Talking with God*, Uhrichsville: Barbour Pubs, 2007.

*Myer, Joyce, *Battlefield of the Mind*, New York: Faith Words, 1995

*Myss, Caroline, *Anatomy of the Spirit*, New York: Harmony Books, 1996.

*Newton, Michael, *Destiny of Souls*, St. Paul: Llewellyn Publications, 2000.

*Newton, Michael, *Journey of Souls,* St. Paul: Llewellyn Publications, 2001.

Osteen, Joel, *Your Best Life Now*, New York: Warner Faith, 2004.

Owen, John, *Spiritual Mindedness*, East Peoria, Versa Press, 1681 & 2009

Owen, John, *The Glory of Christ*, East Peoria, Versa Press, 1684 & 1998

Owen, John, *Searching Difficult Times*, East Peoria, Versa Press, 1721 & 2019

Owen, John, *The Holy Spirit*, East Peoria, Versa Press, 1674 & 2004

Owen, John, *Temptation Resisted*, East Peoria, Versa Press, 1658 & 2020

Owen, John, *Indwelling Sin in Believers*, East Peoria, Versa Press, 1668 & 2010

Owen, John, *Apostasy From the Gospel,* East Peoria, Versa Press, 1676 & 1992

Owen, John, *Communion with God,* East Peoria, Versa Press, 1657 & 1991

Owen, John, *The Mortification of Sin*, East Peoria, Versa Press, 1656 & 2004

Owen, John, *The Spirit and the Church*, East Peoria, Versa Press, 1674 & 2002

Owen, John, *Duties of Christian Fellowship,* East Peoria, Versa Press, 1647 & 2017 –John Owens books above are now published by Banner of Truth Trust

Paluch, Jim. *5 Important Things*, Mechanicsburg: Executive Books, 1996.

Pausch, Randy, *The Last Lecture*, New York: Hyperion, 2008.

Pegues, D. S., *30 Days to Taming Your Tongue*, Eugene: Harvest House, 2005.

Petty, Joe, *Apples of Gold*, New York: Bristol Park Books, 1962.

Pritchett, Price, *The Ethics of Excellence*, Dallas: Pritchett.

*Pritchett, Price, *The Unfolding*, Dallas: Pritchett.

Renard, John, *The Handy Religion Answer Book*, Canton: Visible Ink Press, 2002.

Reed, Anna, *Life of Washington*, Green Forest: Attic Books, 2009.

Sharpe, Kevin, *Sleuthing the Divine*, Minneapolis: Fortress Press, 2000.

Sherman, Doug, *Keeping Your Ethical Edge Sharp*, New York: Nav Press, 1990.

Smith, Huston, *Why Religion Matters*, New York: HarperCollins, 2001.

Stanard, Russell, *God for the 21st Century*, London: Templeton Foundation Press, 2000.

Staniforth, Vincent, *Questions for My Father,* Hillsboro: Beyond Words, 1998.

Bibliography

*Stone, Perry, Secrets of the Third Heaven, Cleveland TN, VOE Ministries, 2020
*Strassman, Rick, M.D, *DMT the Spirit Molecule*, Rochester: Park St. Press, 2001
Swindoll, Charles, *The Owner's Manual for Christians,* Nashville: Thomas Nelson, 2011.
*Swindoll, Charles, *A Life Well Lived*, Nashville: Thomas Nelson, 2007.
Swindoll, Charles, *Laugh Again*, Anaheim, CA, Insight for Living, 1992
*Swinburne, Richard, *The Evolution of the Soul*, NY, Oxford Univ. Press, 2007
Tarnas, Richard, *The Passion of the Western Mind,* NY: Random House, 1991
Tarpey, James. *The Meaning of Life: One Man's Journey...,* Kindle Edition,
Tillich, Paul, *The Courage To Be*, New Haven: Yale University Press, 2000.
*Towns, Elmer, *How to Pray*, Ventura: Regal Books, 2006.
Towns, Elmer, *The Daniel Fast*, Ventura: Regal Books, 2010.
Towns, Elmer, *Fasting for Spiritual Breakthrough,* Ventura: Regal Books, 1996.
Tzu, Lao, *Tao Te Ching*, London: Arcturus, 2009.
Walsch, Neale, *On Holistic Living*, Charlottesville: Hampton Roads Pub, 1999.
Walsch, Neale, *God, Creation, and Tools for Life*, Carlsbad: Hay House, 2000.
*Warren, Rick, *The Purpose Driven Life*, Grand Rapids: Zondervan, 2002.
*Washington, George. *Rules of Civility*, Bedford: Applewood Books, 1988.
Weems, Renita, *Listening for God*, New York: Simon & Schuster, 1999.
Welch, Bob, *52 lessons from a Christmas Carol*, Thomas Nelson, NY, 2015
Wickman, Leslie, *God of the Big Bang*, Brentwood: Worthy Books, 2015.
*Wiese, Bill, *23 Minutes in Hell,* Lake Mary, FL, Charisma House, 2017
Wilkinson, Bruce, *The Dream Giver*, Colorado Springs: Multnomah Books, 2003.
Zadra, Dan, *How Many People Does It Take to Make a Difference?* Seattle: Compendium, 2009.
Zukav, Gary, *The Heart of the Soul*, New York: Simon & Schuster, 2001.
*Zukav, Gary, *The Seat of the Soul*, New York: Simon & Schuster, 1989.
Zwirn, Isidor, *The Rabbi from Burbank*, Fort Worth: Ken Copeland Pubs, 1986.

The following sixty-four college courses, available from the Teaching Company, have been completed in the preparation of this book series. All are available from the Teaching Company at 1-800-832-2412 or at http://www.thegreatcourses.com based in Chantilly, VA 20151.

Course #   Title
PC6111---Augustine
PC452 --- Voltaire
PC616 --- God and Mankind
PC408 --- Ethics of Aristotle
PA455 ---The Quest for Meaning
PC4453---Natural Law
PC470 --- Great Minds 3rd ed.
PC4123---Passions: Philosophy and the Intelligence of Emotions
PC4433---Questions of Value

Bibliography

PC297 --- C.S. Lewis
PC4168---Consciousness and Its Implications
PC463 --- Plato, Socrates, and the Dialogues
PC287 --- Dante's Divine Comedy
PC4600---Books That Have Made History
PD1580---Understanding the Brain
PC6312---Religions of the Axial Age
PC4680---Philosophy of Religion
PC4473---Practical Philosophy
PC893 --- Terror of History
PC4636---Reason & Faith: Philosophy in the Middle Ages
PD3310---Long Shadow of the Ancient Greek World
PD3504---The History of Ancient Egypt
PC4235---Great Philosophical Debates: Free Will and Determinism
PC6240---Jesus and the Gospels
PC6100---Great World Religions, 2nd Edition
PC6121---Introduction to Religion
PC337 --- Famous Greeks
PD1564---The Human Body: How We Fail, How We Heal
PC349 --- Famous Romans
PC1597---Biology and Behavior
PC1620---Psychology of Human Behavior
PC197 --- Human Development
PC1663---Origins of the Human Mind
PC6260---Biblical Wisdom Literature
PC4812---Conservative Tradition
PC1597---Biology and Behavior
PC4610---Philosophy, Religion, and the Meaning of Life
PC4278---Philosophy of Mind
PC4244---Philosophy as a Guide to Living
PC2180---Life Lessons from the Great Books
PC4360---Wisdom of History
PC6810---Why Evil Exists
PC657 --- Apostle Paul
PC1970---Lifelong Health: Achieving Optimum Well-Being at Any Age
PC6380---Confucius, Buddha, Jesus, and Muhammad
PC1585---Stress and Your Body
PC1682---The Spiritual Brain: Science and Religious Experience
PC6433---Apocalypse: Controversies and Meaning in Western History
PC6450---History of Christian Theology
PC6130---Mystical Tradition: Judaism, Christianity, and Islam
PC1933---Practicing Mindfulness: An Introduction to Meditation
PC4413---Understanding the World through Experience

Bibliography

PC6299---History of the Bible
PC4182---Exploring Metaphysics
SA6160---Sacred Texts of the World
SA6650---Biblical Literature
PC4222---Moral Decision Making: How to approach Everyday Ethics
PC6941---The City of God
PC1637---Scientific Secrets for Self-Control
PC1648---Why You Are Who You Are
PC6822---Death, Dying, and the Afterlife
PC4130---The Big Questions of Philosophy
PC1257--- Time: A Mystery of Modern Physics
PD4189---Understanding the Dark Side of Human Nature